The Big Story

As Richard Ashley sat in the hotel lounge in
Sorrento he was savouring in anticipation the
moment every newspaperman dreams about,
the capture of the big story. Within an hour
he would have in his hands photostat copies of
letters revealing a web of graft spread over
Southern Italy, and in the middle of it Vittorio,
Duke of Orgagna. Then the big story blew up,
and Ashley found that in the South truth is as
dangerous to dig up as a landmine, that when
it comes out it is never simple, but complicated
and bloodstained. In the end, on Orgagna's
estate, the truth made its startling appearance.

BOOKS BY

MORRIS WEST

———

FICTION

Gallows on the Sand

Kundu

The Big Story

GENERAL

Children of the Sun

MORRIS WEST

The Big Story

HEINEMANN

MELBOURNE   LONDON   TORONTO

William Heinemann Ltd

LONDON   MELBOURNE   TORONTO

CAPE TOWN   AUCKLAND

THE HAGUE

———

First published 1957

Printed in Great Britain
at The Windmill Press
Kingswood, Surrey

FOR

JOYCE

WITH LOVE AND

GRATITUDE

"It must be considered that there is nothing more difficult to carry out, nor more doubtful of success, nor more dangerous to handle, than to initiate a new order of things. For the reformer has enemies in all those who profit by the old order, and only lukewarm defenders in all those who would profit by the new."

MACHIAVELLI: *The Prince*

CHAPTER ONE

IT WAS THE BIG STORY—the biggest of his life.

He sat at ease in the lounge of the Hotel Caravino savouring it page by careful page, as a general might savour the schedule of his coming triumph, as a woman might savour the letters of a constant lover.

Between the buff manila covers it lay pat, precise and unimpeachable—the story that every newsman dreams of in bed and babbles in his hopeful cups. Nothing was wanting to it but proof and this would be in his hands within the hour, when Enzo Garofano, the informer, came to collect his fee and hand over the photostats of the Orgagna letters.

Then he would leave Sorrento and this bright, tourist paradise with its wall of curtained glass and its dazzling murals and its sun-drenched terrace, and its vista of cliff and sea and brown bodies stretched under the blossoming umbrellas. He would pack and go—back to Rome, back to the office where the teleprinter girls would be waiting to send the story to Paris, to London and New York, where it would burst into shattering headlines in the morning editions.

And under the headlines would be his own name: Our Special Correspondent, Richard Ashley.

He was a big man, tall, broad-shouldered, flat-bellied, with cropped hair and a lean brown face scored about the mouth and eyes with the lines of harsh experience. He was dressed, holiday-fashion, in a loose flowered shirt, blue linen slacks and a pair of espadrilles made by the local craftsmen.

Today, he had reached forty years of age. Even that thought was pleasant to him. A man is fortunate when he comes at one stride to the climacteric and to the climax of his career.

He closed the folder and laid it on the table beside his chair. He looked at his watch. Three-thirty. At four-thirty Garofano would come. Some time in the next hour he must hear from Rome that the office had approved his offer of two thousand dollars for the photostats and that the cash had been lodged with American Express in Sorrento. He frowned with faint impatience. Hansen was running it too fine for comfort.

At the bar, Roberto coughed discreetly. Ashley looked up. Roberto gave him a flashing Latin smile and pointed to the terrace. Ashley followed the gesture and saw a pair of attractive brown legs stretched on the bright cushions of a chaise-longue. The rest of their owner was invisible behind the curtains at the right of the door.

Ashley grinned and shook his head. It was a provocative picture, but to a man on the eve of his triumph it was of no interest at all.

"Keep your mind on your job, Roberto. Fix me a martini. And if this one's not dry enough, I'll pour it down your neck."

Roberto chuckled happily.

"Better than that, give it to the lady and I'll make you another one."

Ashley shrugged away the suggestion.

"I can't afford the time or the money. Besides, I'm working."

Roberto put down the bottle with a thump and gestured theatrically.

"Working! In this sunlight? At this hour? In the presence of such beauty? *Vergogna!*"

He sighed mightily, and bent to the rituals of measuring drinks and slicing lemon-peel behind the bright tiles of the bar-front. He was a dark, compact fellow, with sleek hair and a small moustache and a pearly smile. He was a good barman. His manner was a discreet combination of deference and Neapolitan insolence. The deference brought him tips from the men and the women paid in different coin for the flattery of insolence.

Ashley looked at his watch again.

"What time does the Post Office open?"

"Three o'clock, *signore.*"

"I'm expecting a telegram. The damn thing should be here by now."

Roberto shrugged philosophically.

"*Pazienza*, my friend! *Pazienza!* First the telegram

3

must arrive at the Post Office. Then it must be copied. Then they must send a messenger to . . ."

He broke off and gaped, goggle-eyed, as the brown legs swung themselves off the chaise-longue and their owner came into view, a blonde in a Capri bathing suit, standing in conscious grace against the balustrade. She smiled, flirted her hips at them and walked out of view towards the end of the terrace.

"Well!"

Roberto beat his forehead in anguish.

"It is too much, *signore!* It is ten times too much! I am married with three children. My wife is expecting another. There is my job which I must keep and my honour which I would lose all too gladly. And I am subjected to temptations like this!"

"I'm thirsty," said Ashley.

"*Subito, signore!*" said Roberto, a wise fellow who knew when a joke was done with.

He lifted the flap of the bar and came towards Ashley with the drink balanced on a small silver tray. He wiped the table, laid down a cardboard chaser, set down the drink with studied care and waited.

"How much?"

"Six hundred lire, *signore*."

Ashley looked up sharply.

"Six hundred? It was four-fifty at lunch-time."

"A mistake, *signore*," said Roberto, blandly. "I meant, of course, to say four-fifty."

"You're a liar, Roberto."

4

Roberto shrugged and smiled, cheerfully.

"You force me to admit it, *signore*. I am a very great liar."

"Why do you lie to me? I tip you well, don't I?"

"Very well, *signore*."

"Then why lie to me?"

"Force of habit, *signore*."

"A bad habit, Roberto."

"Let us call it a disease of the profession." Roberto cocked a quizzical eye at Ashley. "Do you never lie, *signore*?"

The question took him by surprise. Roberto was still smiling, but there was a new note in his voice, an odd fugitive expression in his dark eyes. It was as if he said, 'We should understand each other, you and I. We have interests in common. We may be of use to each other.'

Ashley answered the question with some care.

"I lie sometimes, yes. But never about money."

"Because you do not need to worry about money. I, on the contrary, must worry about it all the time. Each of us lies about the thing that is important to him."

And there it was, the opening gambit, laid down for him in the Neapolitan fashion with smiles and circumlocutions. Roberto had something to tell him, but he was not prepared to tell it without payment. The next move was up to Ashley.

"What do you think is important to me, Roberto?"

Roberto cocked his head on one side in the fashion of the South.

"This telegram which you expect. The information which is contained in that book——" he pointed down at the manila folder, "—and the man who is coming to see you at four-thirty this afternoon!"

It shocked him like water dashed in the face. He started forward and the glass rocked perilously on the table. Then he took control of himself and sat back in the chair. He looked at Roberto. The dark eyes told him nothing. They were blank as a bird's. Cautiously, Ashley framed the next question.

"The book, I can understand—you've seen me working on it. The telegram—I spoke about that myself. But the other—the visitor I'm expecting—how and what do you know about him?"

"The drink," said Roberto, flatly. "The *signore* has not paid for his drink."

Ashley fished in his hip pocket for his wallet. He took out a five-thousand lire note and laid it deliberately on the silver tray. Roberto's eyes brightened. He picked up the note, folded it slowly and put it away.

"It is a message, *signore*," he said, softly. "It says that the man who comes to see you is a liar and a cheat. You should take what he offers but trust him not at all."

"Anything else?"

"Nothing else."

He picked up the tray and walked back to the bar. Ashley sat back in his chair and watched him go. He made no argument. He asked no more questions. He knew that he might talk till doomsday and still not prise another particle of information from those subtle smiling lips.

Besides, he was not too perturbed. He had been too long and too deeply involved in this investigation not to know that the Italian thrives on gossip and theatrical intrigue. At each stage of his story he had been beset by contact men and pedlars of useless information. They would button-hole him in bars and press clubs and hotel foyers; they would come introduced by friends or simply because they had heard that the '*scrittore Americano*' was prepared to pay for information. They would talk largely and vaguely of sinister doings and dangerous influences—and end always with a plea for advance money. Sometimes a few grains of truth sifted out of their talk. Most often it blew away in chaff and husks.

Then they would try to sell him other things—warnings of attempts on his life, names and addresses of men who might offer him protection. He did not blame them too much. In Italy a man had to live as best he could—by peddling gossip to the press or peddling charm to dowager tourists. But he was not prepared to fret about them. He had tested the fabric of his story. It was too strong to be shaken by anything but catastrophe.

So he told himself as he sat in his chair and sipped his drink and flipped again through the pages of his manuscript. But a faint unease still nagged at him. A small sourness had crept into the sweet taste of his triumph.

He weighed Roberto's message again.

"The man who comes to see you is a liar and a cheat." Nothing new in that. Garofano was a cheap huckster, peddling stolen documents. He must be a liar and he must be a cheat. But the documents were genuine enough. He had seen them and studied them. They fitted like joiners' pieces into the framework of his evidence.

"Take what he offers, but trust him not at all." What he offered was a physical commodity—photostatic copies of documents already inspected and verified. There was no possibility of forgery. The question of trust did not arise.

There were only two questions of any importance. The identity of the messenger and the reason for the warning. Even to these there was an obvious answer— profit! Five thousand lire splits neatly in half. Half to the barman, half to a seedy tout who has heard gossip in a bar. The '*scrittore Americano*' is buying something from Enzo Garofano. Pass him a friendly warning and we share the tip. A simple version of the skin game, which the Neapolitans call *la combinazione!*

Ashley grinned wryly at the butt-end of the thought. He began to feel better. Then the page-boy came in with a telegram.

Ashley paid him and dismissed him, then tore open the shoddy yellow envelope. The message was brief and blunt:

AUTHORISE INFORMATION PAYMENT TWO THOUSAND

8

DOLLARS STOP CURRENCY AVAILABLE AMERICAN EXPRESS
SORRENTO STOP ADVISE CONCLUSION DEAL . . . HANSEN.

Good! He smiled grimly, crumpled the message form and thrust it into his pocket. Rome had approved. The money was available. Now there was nothing to do but wait for Enzo Garofano. He tossed off his drink and walked out into the raw sunlight of the terrace.

Roberto watched him with cool and speculative eyes.

The girl watched him, too.

She saw his chiselled, lean face and the big frame of him and the strong hands and the easy relaxation of his walk. She saw how he leaned on the balustrade and looked down at the bright huts and the baking bodies on the beach, then out across the blue water to the blurred outline of Naples and the misty shapes of Ischia and Procida. He had the attitude of a man at ease with himself and with the world, a man with time to spend. There were good reasons why he should be induced to spend some of it on her.

She leaned back against the angle of the railing, sucking in her belly and thrusting up her chest as a model does for a photographer; then she twitched the bright beach-stole about her so that the flash of colour would catch his eye. When he turned, she smiled at him and heard him greet her in English:

"Good day there!"

"*Buon giorno . . . Va bene così nel sole!*"

The Italian greeting surprised him. Because she was

9

blonde with a honey-coloured tan, he had taken her for a foreigner. American, perhaps, like himself, or a Swede or a Gretchen from the Rhineland.

"*Italiana?*"

"*Si, Italiana. Da Roma.*"

She smiled and gestured for him to join her at the end of the terrace. From Rome? That might mean anything. Venice, Trento, Florence, Pisa. The blonde Lombard stock had filtered far and wide through the peninsula. His tongue slipped easily into the cadence of the language and they talked, facing each other across the angle of the terrace, while the voices and the music drifted up faintly from the beach, two hundred feet below.

They were pleased with each other, piqued with interest to learn a little more. The familiar prelude played itself comfortably, question by question.

"You're new here? I haven't seen you before."

"I arrived late last night. And you?"

"Oh, I've been here a week—ten days."

"On holiday?"

"Not exactly. Working."

"A nice place to work. What do you do?"

"I'm a correspondent—a newsman."

"Interesting. That means you travel, write stories, meet many people. A good life."

"Sometimes." It was a good life now, on the day of his fortieth birthday, with his masterwork an hour from completion, with a blonde beauty smiling at him in the

sun, and the small disquiet pushed comfortably to the
back of his mind. "By the way, my name's Ashley . . .
Richard Ashley."

"Elena Carrese."

He liked the way she said it, simply, comfortably,
with none of the coy, come-hither blushes of the Neapolitan girls.

"Are you holidaying too?"

"For today only. My employer arrives tomorrow."

"Oh!" The prelude jarred and jangled into discord.
Girls whose bosses gave them suites at the Caravino,
were very special girls indeed.

"In the winter we work in Rome. In the summer
we come down here." It came out smoothly, without
hesitation or embarrassment.

"Lucky people," said Ashley, dryly. "What sort of
work do you—I mean does your employer do?"

She made a wide and careful gesture so that the wrap
fell away from her shoulders and Ashley had to bend
close to her to retrieve it.

"What does he do? Oh . . . many things, politics,
investment, banking . . . He travels a good deal. So,
naturally, I travel too."

"Naturally. Come to think of it, I'd probably know
him."

"Probably." There was no malice in her eyes, no hint
of irony in her smile. "If you are a correspondent, you
may even have met him. He is quite famous in Italy."

"What's his name?"

"Vittorio, Duke of Orgagna."

Well for a man that he has played poker at the cable desk for the young years of his life! Well for a man that he has charmed stories from the Ambassador's typist, while his colleagues were drinking the Ambassador's sherry! Well for a man that he has come to forty years and learned to control his face muscles while his stomach cramps with sudden fear! Richard Ashley made a little comedy of surprise and deference and said:

"Orgagna? Of course! I've interviewed him several times."

He might have said: 'I know this Orgagna better than you will ever know him, sweetheart. You work for him. You may even share his bed. But I have lived his past and his present. I am the arbiter of his dubious future. I know how much money he has and how he came by it. I know the stretch of his power and the limit of his influence. I know the men he has bought. I have traded with those who are selling him in their turn. I know the woman he married and the others he has loved—all except you, sweetheart, who are something of a surprise to me. I have tallied his triumphs and today I shall compass his final defeat. Tomorrow I shall publish his damnation to the world.'

He might have said it, but he didn't. Instead he grinned, an engaging crooked grin, arranged the stole over the sleek shoulders of Elena Carrese and told her:

"Tomorrow you belong to Orgagna. Today, you belong to me. It's my birthday and I've had good news.

I'd like to celebrate. Will you have a drink with me?"

"*Senz'altro, signore!* Certainly!" said Elena Carrese, and, swaying her lithe body against him, she walked into the lounge.

The radio was playing softly '*A'nnamurata Mia*' and Roberto was polishing glasses and ranging them on the black glass shelves of the bar. He looked up as they entered and his face broke into a goatish smile of approval when he saw the girl.

They settled themselves on the high stools at the bar and ordered drinks. They made a laughing little ceremony out of the toasts. Ashley made extravagant compliments in Neapolitan, and she pouted prettily and said "*Vergogna!*" and let her hand rest for a moment on his own. It was all so frank and charming and natural —a holiday encounter in the Siren Land.

Or was every line of it an elaborate lie?

For more than six months he had been dredging the murky waters of Italian politics and finance. Impossible to make a secret of an operation like that. Incredible that Orgagna himself should remain ignorant of the man who was investigating him. Equally incredible that this climactic day should pass without some action to prevent publication of his indictment. Perhaps this meeting with Elena Carrese was the beginning of it.

But she was still smiling at him, still chattering and making her pretty mannequin gestures.

"You told me you had good news?"

"News?" His mind was far away. "Oh—oh yes."

"You have not yet told me what it is."

'Now,' he thought, 'now we come to the core of it. *Piano, piano . . .!* Softly, in the Italian way, we come to it. Tell me your news, kind sir, so that I may tell it to my master who is Vittorio, Duke of Orgagna.' He shrugged in deprecation.

"Oh . . . it's just one of those professional things. I've written a news story which turned out to be a good story. My paper has just given me permission to buy certain documents. Now, I have a very good story."

"What sort of a story is it?" Her eyes were wide and innocent.

"Political."

"Oh!" said Elena Carrese, and the little exclamation hung like a suspended chord of music.

"When we get to know each other better, I'll tell you about it."

"A singular indiscretion," said a flat English voice.

Ashley swung round with an angry exclamation and his drink slopped over the bar. The girl turned too and they saw before them a small dapper fellow with a bland, boyish face and mild eyes. He was dressed in the English fashion, in a blue reefer jacket, grey slacks, a silk shirt and a meticulous foulard scarf. He had the incongruous youthful air of those born under a cold star. Ignoring Ashley's obvious displeasure, he moved towards the bar. Elena Carrese watched him warily. He held out his hand in greeting.

"Ashley, my dear chap, so nice to see you."

"Sure . . . very nice." Ashley gave him an indifferent handshake and an indifferent introduction. "Elena Carrese—George Harlequin."

Harlequin nodded casually to the girl and turned back to Ashley.

"We seem to run across each other everywhere, don't we?"

"Don't we!"

"Press club in Venice, spring festival in Florence, Joe's Bar and Grill, Rome, Stampa in Naples. And now here. Odd really."

"Very."

Abruptly, George Harlequin switched to Italian. He bowed ironically to the girl and said:

"You're looking very beautiful, Lena."

"Thank you," said the girl, without enthusiasm.

"Do you two know each other?" Ashley was surprised and cautious.

"We have met," said Elena, stiffly. She slid quickly off the stool and turned away from the bar. "Excuse me, I must go."

"Look, you can't just . . ."

"Please excuse me." Already she was half-way to the door.

"Will you have dinner with me tonight?"

"I'm sorry. It is impossible."

"After dinner, then—coffee?"

She had reached the door. In a moment she would be gone. Then she halted and turned back.

"Very well then, after dinner—coffee."

Then she was gone and George Harlequin was perched on the stool, chuckling like a pixie. Ashley was blazing with anger.

"All right, Harlequin, let's have it. You've been dogging my tracks for months. Now we've both come to the end of the line. What do you want?"

"First, I'd like a drink," said George Harlequin coolly.

"Name it."

"Scotch and water."

"*Subito, signore,*" said Roberto.

"We'll drink at the table."

Ashley moved across to the small coffee-table where his manuscript still lay in its stiff manila cover. Harlequin followed him and Roberto watched them warily as he poured the drinks. The Englishman lit a cigarette and smoked quietly until the glasses were set on the table and Roberto had retired discreetly to his cubbyhole at the end of the bar. Then he raised his glass, grinning at Ashley over the rim.

"Good luck, Ashley!"

"Damn your eyes!" Ashley drained his drink at a gulp and set the glass down on the table. "Okay, Harlequin, let's have it, chapter and verse. Who are you? What do you want—and why?"

Harlequin's eyes were mild and deceptive. His mouth twisted in wry distaste.

"I think you know the answers already."

"I'd like to hear them from you."

The little man shrugged and laid his cigarette carefully on the lip of the ash-tray.

"Very well." He laid his hands together, finger-tip to finger-tip, in a fastidious gesture. "For the past six months you've been preparing an indictment."

"I've been building a news story."

"Which is, in effect, an indictment of certain Italian politicians for fraud, gerrymandering and misappropriation of dollar relief funds."

"Check."

"It's an impressive piece of work, Ashley."

"You've read it, of course," said Ashley, with heavy irony.

"I have indeed," said George Harlequin genially. "Every line, even the marginal additions."

Ashley stared at him in hostile surprise.

"The hell you have!"

"For a long-service professional, you've been very careless with your papers."

Ashley thrust himself forward across the table. His eyes were narrow. His mouth was grim.

"What the devil are you?"

"A professional."

"Professional what?"

Harlequin waved an airy hand.

"Contact man, courier, negotiator . . ."

"Agent?"

"Call it any name you like."

"Whom do you represent?"

"The Government of Her Britannic Majesty. Er—unofficially, of course."

"So that's it!"

Ashley leaned back in his chair and laughed. The tension in him relaxed. The taste of triumph was sweet again on his tongue. The big story was bigger than he had dreamed. The dovecotes were fluttering in Whitehall. Tomorrow they would be squawking in panic at the headlines. Doubt and uncertainty fell away from him. He prepared to enjoy the comedy.

"You make me feel very important, Harlequin. Why should the British Government be interested in me?"

"You're buying the Orgagna photostats, aren't you?"

Ashley's eyes hardened. He felt uneasy again.

"So you know about those, too?"

"Naturally."

"Okay, then! I'm buying them. I'm buying them in say twenty minutes from now, in this room, at this table."

"Then your indictment will be complete?"

"Complete. The big men and the little ones will be arraigned at the bar of public opinion. The photostats are final and conclusive evidence of one of the biggest politico-financial scandals of the twentieth century, planned and executed by His Excellency the Duke of Orgagna."

"Pity," said George Harlequin, with donnish distaste.

18

"A very great pity! When will you run the story?"

"I imagine it will break the day after tomorrow. It's quite timely. The Italian elections are only ten days off."

"The Americans have a great sense of theatre," said Harlequin regretfully. He heaved himself out of the chair, walked over to the door that led on to the terrace and stood looking out across the sunlit water. Then he turned back. "Mind if we talk out here? It's a little more private."

"Just as you like."

Ashley picked up the manuscript folder and walked out on to the terrace. Harlequin began to pace slowly up and down the long cat-walk slung out over two hundred feet of bright emptiness. Ashley fell into step beside him. The little man was not smiling now. His air of urbane mockery had dropped away like an actor's cloak. His voice was sober and thoughtful.

"Ashley, I think you understand the political situation in this country. There is an extreme Left wing, strong and well-organised. There is a small, but highly capitalised reactionary Right. There is a weak coalition of the Centre—the moderates of both groups who hold the governing votes."

"That's right."

"It is to the interest of Europe, it is to the interest of Great Britain and America, to maintain and strengthen this coalition of the Centre."

"Right again."

"The man who has held them together so far is Orgagna."

"I don't agree," said Ashley, with blunt conviction.

Harlequin took it calmly enough. It was as if he were at pains to avoid an open breach.

"Let us say then, that, in the opinion of some—in the opinion of my government—Orgagna is the key to unity. He has connections with the Right and the Left. He is a skilled negotiator. He has a certain dash which goes down well with the public. Take him away and you are left with mediocrities. You see?"

Ashley flared into sudden anger.

"I see damn well! You're asking me to kill this story so that an expert in grand larceny can hold a portfolio in the Italian Government." He laughed bitterly. "That's a hell of a line for one professional to hand to another."

The bland, boyish face smiled disarmingly.

"It's the only line I have, Ashley. If I could bribe you, I would. If I could blackmail you, I'd do that, too. In the present circumstances I have no other argument than the truth. I'm using it to the best of my ability."

Ashley stopped in his tracks and faced him.

"Fine! I admit your sincerity. Now I'll tell you what you're really asking. You want me to suppress a criminal act—a whole series of criminal acts—for the sake of a political expedient."

"You might put it that way, yes! But I'd like to add

a rider—a political expedient on which the stability of European defence may depend."

Ashley gaped at him a moment, then burst out:

"God, how I love the British! They are the most moral nation in the world—the Royal family, the Established Church and the sacred rituals of cricket! Yet their whole history is founded on economic immoralities and political expedients! Their heroes are pirates and filibusters. Their saints are eccentrics and anarchists. They preach morals on the floor of the House and plot their wars in the Conservative Club. They rail against Wall Street and American expansionism and their business-men are buccaneers in striped pants! And when they slip up, they invoke the Old Pals Act and the bonds of British Brotherhood. For God's sake, Harlequin!"

Harlequin was unmoved by the outburst. He said, mildly:

"It's an extreme view and now is not the time to argue it. I think we're talking at cross purposes, my dear chap."

"I don't think so."

"You're talking about morals. I'm talking about politics. The two are mutually exclusive."

"That's a fallacy and you know it."

"I don't think it is. Politics is the art and science of governing imperfect men through imperfect systems."

"It's bad politics to put false men and venal men in positions of power."

"Not always. False men can be directed. Venal men can be bought. It is the diplomat's job to profit from the fear of the liar and the greed of the peculator."

"And the truth?"

"The truth?" George Harlequin shrugged wryly. "The truth, my dear Ashley, is a luxury available only to those who are not involved in its consequences."

"Meaning what?"

"Meaning that you, personally, are not involved in Italy, nor in Europe for that matter. Your story can tip this tottering government off its pedestal, can plunge this country into economic and political chaos, can upset years of staff-work on European defence and Mediterranean strategy. And you yourself can fly next week to India or Java or Australia and feel no consequence in your body or your soul."

"And you, of course, are involved?" Ashley grinned at him sardonically.

Quietly and carefully the small man measured out his answer.

"As a professional, yes. I am not an observer, as you are. I am a participant. I am involved because my country is involved, because I live thirty miles from the shores of Europe, and the politics of Europe determine whether I have dry toast or devilled kidneys for breakfast. You are the press—the peripatetic truth-pedlars. I am the man who must live with lies and make terms with injustice and compromise with corruption, because these are constant elements in human society."

"You, and men like you, perpetuate injustice by coming to terms with it."

"And men like you?"

"We're involved, too," said Ashley slowly. "We're involved because we see, more than you, more often than you, the consequences of lies and injustice. We see starvation in the streets, while you read about it in a white paper. We see murder done and send you photographs to prove it. We see children shot and women raped six months before you read a ten-line memorandum about a border incident. We're involved, make no mistake. We're involved, because in our wrong-headed way we believe there's honour in peddling the truth. Even Socrates managed to make quite a reputation at it."

"And was poisoned for his pains."

"We accept that as a professional risk." Ashley shrugged wearily and leaned back against the iron balustrade. "All this gets us nowhere. The position is quite simple. You, or your government, want to put Orgagna in the Cabinet. I want to put him in gaol. Your motive is political expedience. Mine is truth."

"Is that your only motive, Ashley?"

"Name me another."

Coolly, precisely, George Harlequin laid down his answer.

"You are—or were—in love with Orgagna's wife!"

CHAPTER TWO

IT WAS AS BRUTAL as a smack in the mouth.

For one wild moment, Ashley wanted to leap at the small fellow, batter his face with his fists and then hurl him out into the emptiness between the blue sky and the blue sea. Instead he leaned backwards, closing his eyes and holding tightly to the bars of the balustrade so that the corroded metal bit into his palms. He was sick with anger. His belly knotted and his tongue seemed too big for his mouth.

Slowly, painfully, he took possession of himself and when he opened his eyes, George Harlequin was still standing before him, staring at him with sombre eyes. Then Ashley found voice.

"You cold-blooded little bastard! You miserable little muck-raker! I haven't seen Cosima for more than ten years. I loved her, yes! I still do. She was my mistress, but I would have married her! Instead she chose Orgagna. I wished her joy and tried to forget her. She has no more to do with my indictment of Orgagna than the man in the moon."

"As his wife, she's involved in it."

"She's his wife. Not mine."

"I wish," said Harlequin, gravely, "I wish I could be

as sure of my motives as you are of yours. You're a fortunate fellow, Ashley. I—I'm sorry I said that. I apologise."

He held out his hand. Ashley rejected the gesture.

"Save it!"

Harlequin shrugged ruefully.

"I take it then you're going ahead with your story."

"I'm going ahead," said Ashley, with grim satisfaction. "I'm going to publish it, chapter, verse and photostats. I'm going to prove that children are dying in the back streets of Naples because Vittorio Orgagna put American relief funds into his own pockets. I'm going to prove that there are two hundred thousand unemployed from Naples to Eboli, because Orgagna and his colleagues diverted reconstruction dollars to his enterprises in the North. I'm going to prove that grain seed from America was sold to party members instead of being distributed to peasant farmers as a gift, and that the man who engineered the sale was Vittorio Orgagna. I'm going to publish the balance sheets of his enterprises and the size of his secret credits in American banks. And you and the people who sent you can go to hell!"

"You're playing with fire."

"I'm not playing."

The little man's shoulders sagged wearily. His boyish face seemed suddenly grey and old. He turned away; then, as if on a sudden impulse, he came back and faced Ashley.

"Let me give you one piece of advice. This is an old,

old country with a turbulent history. There is violence in it and corruption and intrigue and political assassination. The family of Orgagna has been part of that history for a good many centuries. Watch yourself, my dear fellow. Watch yourself! And if you think better of your decision, come to me."

"I'll see you in hell first."

"It's a strong possibility," said Harlequin softly.

Then he was gone and Ashley was left alone, perched on his stone cat-walk high over the summer sea.

Muted by the distance, the sounds drifted up to him: the shouts of the brown boys, the high laughter of the girls, the splash of the divers from the jetty, the tinny radios blaring Neapolitan songs, the *put-put* of a cruising pleasure boat. It was playtime in the South—time of the siren-song, season of the dancing fauns. The wise were those who spent their days in the sun and their nights making love under the orange trees or on the warm sands under the tufa cliffs. Only a fool, like himself, would waste his days and his nights raking over the embers of another man's sins.

He asked himself, which of the drowsing thousands on the sands would read the story he had written for them. Which of them, having read it, would thank him for the service?

'Why write it then? Why put your life in jeopardy and your soul in the way of damnation in the sacred name of news? Is a by-line worth a life? Is a revolution worth an hour on the beach with a willing girl?

26

'The truth? A sacred dedication but a thankless service. Justice? A blind goddess whose scales never quite swing true. Pride? Ambition? Vanity? All of them drive a man but none of them quite explain him.

'You chose a profession in which you hoped to excel. You enjoyed its rewards. You accepted its limitations. You shared responsibility for its sins. A man and his works must be judged in the state and station to which he belongs. Even God Almighty tempers absolute justice with infinite mercy.

'Then if you judge yourself with so much clemency, why not Vittorio, Duke of Orgagna?

'He, too, was born in a state and to a station. He was born out of a thousand years of intrigue into an old and corrupt country. His profession is statecraft and the manipulation of money. He, too, must be judged in his own *milieu* and in the shadow of his own history. Can you judge him thus, justly? If not, by what right do you pen his condemnation?'

It was a new and uneasy thought, but before he had time to pursue it, the telephone rang and he walked back into the airy coolness of the lounge. Roberto was talking to the reception desk.

"*Pronto! . . . Come si chiama?* Garofano? . . . *Aspett'un moment'.*" He looked up at Ashley. "Signore Ashley, there is a gentleman to see you. His name is Garofano."

"Ask them to send him in."

Roberto spoke again into the phone:

"*Il signore aspetta nella salone. Si, si, subito!*" He put

27

down the receiver and turned to Ashley. "He is coming now, *signore*. You will want drinks? I have tourists to serve in the other room and . . ."

"No drinks. Just two coffees."

"Two coffees? That will take a few minutes, *signore*."

"We'll wait."

Roberto bowed himself out of the room and, a moment later, Enzo Garofano came in.

He was a thin, dark, seedy fellow with a narrow face and darting eyes set too close to his nose. He was dressed in the current Neapolitan fashion—short, tight coat, stove-pipe trousers and shiny pointed shoes. He walked lightly and jerkily and his movements were nervous and furtive. He carried a battered brief-case under his arm.

"Nice to see you, Garofano," said Ashley cheerfully. He held out his hand. Garofano gave him a limp handshake but said nothing. He eased himself into a chair, propped his brief-case against the table-leg and began mopping his face with a soiled handkerchief. Then he put the handkerchief away and fumbled for a cigarette. Ashley offered him one from his own case and lit it for him. Garofano puffed greedily for a few moments. His hands were trembling.

"Relax, relax!" said Ashley, easily. "It's all over. We'll have some coffee and finish the business in five minutes. Er—have you got the photostats?"

"No."

Ashley almost leapt from his chair.

"What?"

"Please, please!" Garofano fluttered nervous hands. "You must not misunderstand me. I mean to say that I do not have them here. I can get them in a moment. It is, you understand, a matter of caution."

"Careful little guy, aren't you?"

"In business—this sort of business—one has to be careful. You—you have heard from your principals?"

"I have. It's good news for both of us. They've agreed to pay."

"How much?"

"The asking price—two thousand dollars in American currency."

"I see."

There was a pause. Enzo Garofano looked down at the backs of his hands and at the small spiral of smoke curling up from the cigarette between his stained and dirty fingers. Puzzled and wary, Ashley watched him. After a moment, Garofano looked up. His hands were not trembling any more. His eyes were steady and he was smiling—the smug, subtle smile of the huckster in a profitable situation. He said, softly:

"I am sorry, my friend. The price has gone up."

Ashley's eyes were bleak.

"How much now?"

"Ten thousand."

"Any reason?"

"The market is lively. I have had a better offer."

"From whom?"

Garofano looked down again at his hands. His eyes were hooded and his voice was touched with ironic regret.

"It is not business to disclose the names of one's clients, *signore*!"

"Business!" Ashley exploded into anger. He heaved himself out of his chair, hoisted Garofano by his lapels and slammed him against the wall. He was babbling with fury, in a mixture of English and gutter Italian. "Business, you say! Business! And then you come along with your cheap shyster tricks. We made a deal —two thousand dollars! I've kept my part of it. Put the money on the line. And by the living God you're going to keep yours if I have to kill you to . . ."

There was a crash of crockery as Roberto came in, dropped the coffee-tray and stood wringing his hands and moaning in despair as Ashley slapped and hammered the helpless fellow pinned against the wall.

"*Signore!* For the love of God! *Basta!* Enough! Enough!"

But Ashley was blind and deaf and he held the struggling, squealing informer and cursed and slapped him until a woman's voice cut across the shouting fury:

"Stop it, Richard! Stop it!"

As Ashley swung round, Garofano wrenched himself free, scooped up his brief-case, and scuttled from the room.

Then he saw her, tall, dark, lovely, standing in the doorway to the terrace—Cosima d'Orgagna. Panting

30

and dishevelled he stood there, staring at her stupidly—the old love, out of the old forgotten time.

"Cosima!"

Roberto stood gaping amid the wreckage of the coffee-cups. Then she spoke again:

"You! *Cameriere!* Clean up this mess and leave us!"

"*Subito, signora!*" Roberto bent swiftly to the voice of authority, gathered up the broken crockery, mopped the dark stains from the carpet and hurried from the room. Ashley stood like a man in a dream, staring at Cosima d'Orgagna.

Then she came to him. She kissed him lightly and began mopping his face, straightening his shirt, chiding him in the old familiar way.

"Richard! Richard! The same brawling, troublesome Richard Ashley! Who was that horrible little fellow? What was the story this time? Here, sit down and compose yourself. Mother of God! But you have not changed at all."

She forced him back into a chair, took cigarettes from her handbag, lit one for him and let him smoke a while, till his eyes cleared and his hands were steady and the madness of the moment was past.

"Now, tell me, Richard."

Ashley passed a weary hand over his eyes and grinned, ruefully.

"It—it doesn't matter. I was buying information from him. We'd fixed a price and, at the last minute, he raised the ante. I went for him."

31

She chuckled and laid an affectionate hand on his own.

"The old Richard! *Testa dura!* The hard-head, beating his brains out over the follies and scandals of the world. You never had much patience, had you?"

"I certainly haven't much now."

"What was the story this time?"

"The story . . .?"

Then he remembered that the story involved her, too, because she was no longer the lover of Richard Ashley, but the wife of Vittorio, Duke of Orgagna. He remembered that without the photostats, he had no story. He remembered the cryptic warning of Roberto and the meeting with Elena Carrese. He knew then that the arrival of Cosima d'Orgagna was no chance, but part of a well-laid plan to prevent the publication of her husband's indictment. How far she was involved he did not know. But he must know—quickly—or see his triumph snatched from him at the last moment.

"The story? It doesn't matter now that you're here. How did you come? When did you arrive? What brings you?"

"I live here, Richard," she told him, simply. "My husband has property on the peninsula. We have a summer villa over by the Cape."

"Oh! Is your husband here, too?"

"He comes down from Rome this evening. We dine and spend the night in the hotel and go up to the villa in the morning."

They looked at each other across the table. Her eyes were soft, her lips were willing. Old memories stirred about his heart-strings. But he was forty years of age and he had learned to be cautious. He said, tentatively:

"We could have an hour or two together then?"

She smiled and said:

"If you want it, yes."

He thought quickly: 'Not here, in the hotel, with Roberto and Harlequin and Elena Carrese. Not after the scandalous brawl with Garofano. Not with Orgagna coming and the servants whispering in broom-cupboards and along the corridors.'

"Have you a car, Cosima?"

"Yes."

"Let's drive somewhere."

"Up the mountain? It's lonely there, and quiet. We can talk—and remember."

"Let's go."

Roberto, coming back through the hall, saw them walk out of the lounge together. He saw Ashley pause at the desk, seal his manuscript in a large envelope and lodge it in the hotel safe-deposit. He saw them step out into the sunlight, hand in hand, like a pair of lovers.

He walked swiftly into the bar and picked up the telephone.

Ashley swung the big blue Isotta out of the hotel drive-way and nosed it carefully through the narrow cobbled alleys towards the centre of the town. When they came to the square, the afternoon buses were decanting their loads of trippers and the carriage-drivers were pulling out from their stand opposite the Bagatelle. The clop of hooves and the tinkle of their little silver bells blended with the blare of horns and the clatter of the hotel touts squabbling over the luggage. Ashley drove slowly through the press of people and headed up the Corso to the grey shoulder of the Cape.

It was not until they were over the hump, winding upward through the olive groves, with the huddled towns and the sea falling away behind them, that Cosima spoke:

"It's like old times, Richard."

"Old times, yes."

The old times were ten years away, when the war was a year-old memory and Richard Ashley still had his milk-teeth and Cosima Benedetto was a wide-eyed girl glad of her first job at the Office, grateful for a man's arms about her and a meal-ticket after the hunger of the locust-years. The old times were the good times—an airy little apartment on Parioli, before the rent sharks moved in, afternoons in the Tivoli gardens, dinner at the pavement restaurants, Sunday driving to Frascati and Ostia and an occasional week-end in Florence or Venice. The old times were the passionate times, when love seemed more than enough and a marriage licence an unnecessary investment. Then he had been sent to Berlin, for relief duty, they told him. But they kept him there more than a year; and while he was there came the letter from Cosima telling him that the old times were over, that she must look to her future, that she was going to marry a man with an income and an old and noble title. He didn't blame her then. He didn't blame her now. There were too many workless men in Italy, too many rootless fellows like himself who enjoyed Latin passion but had no mind to marry it.

Old times . . . old ghosts! But the ghosts were not laid yet and the old love was here at his side, windblown and beautiful, climbing up the last slopes to the spine of the Sorrentine peninsula.

"Did you hate me, Richard?"

"Hate you? No. I'm still a little in love with you, I think."

"That's nice to hear."

'Nice to hear. Easy to say. But dangerous, too. Love her you may, but surrender to her you cannot. Not now or ever again. She is the key to mysteries. You must use her against Orgagna as Orgagna would use her against you.'

Staring ahead through the windscreen at the flaring blue of the sky, Ashley felt suddenly ashamed of himself.

A tiny donkey cart came pattering round the bend and Ashley wrenched the big car over to avoid a collision. Cosima gasped and flung herself against him and he was aware of the disturbing nearness of her body and the perfume of her hair. Then they swung round the curve, and saw on the summit of the rise a ruined chapel, framed by olive trees.

35

"We'll stop there, Richard."

"Anywhere you like."

"The locals call it 'Il Deserto'—the retreat. Appropriate, isn't it?"

"Very."

He pulled the car off the road and it bumped and swayed over the rutted track that led to the ancient chapel. They stopped. He helped Cosima out of the car and they stood together on the high saddle of the mountain, listening to the shrill chorus of the cicadas and the rare, lost piping of a bird.

The beauty of it was breath-taking. On the one side was the bay of Naples, with the white towns and the orange groves that started at the cliffs' edge and scrambled up the hillside to where the woods began. On the other was the bay of Salerno, where the hills were steeper and the towns were rarer and the blossom trees grew out of the bodies of dead men.

"Richard?"

"Yes?"

"I—I am glad you still love me a little."

"Why?"

"I have much need of love."

In the old time he would have taken her in his arms and crushed her mouth with kisses. But he was wiser now and warier. He held her, lightly with his arm about her shoulders, and grinned a little crookedly and said:

"I offered it to you once."

"It was less important to me then."

"Than what?" His voice was harsh and he felt her stiffen against him. "Than a noble marriage?"

"Than the certainty of eating when the great correspondent grew tired of his little Roman mistress and went away."

Her frankness put him on the defensive. The ground he had hoped to gain was lost already. She drew away from him and he turned to face her. He said, quietly, almost humbly:

"You never told me you wanted to be married."

She gave him a bitter little smile.

"Would it have mattered if I had?"

"It mattered afterwards."

She shrugged and stared away over the blue water.

"Afterwards is always an hour too late. It was too late for me also."

He was uncertain of her now. This was no careful comedy of seduction played to protect her husband. She was remote from him and hurt and cold. He bent down and plucked a sprig of grass and began tearing it to pieces with restless fingers.

"I hoped you might have married happily."

"I married well. I got no less than I expected."

"What did you get?"

She faced him then, bright-eyed and defiant, her voice a chill mockery.

"Everything a noble Italian can offer to his wife—except love and fidelity."

"You've missed quite a lot."

"No more than most who make the same bargain. Men like my husband have a nice sense of justice. They demand pleasure from professionals, passion from their mistresses and discretion from their wives. They are prepared to pay for all three."

"Do they never try to combine the talents?" He grinned, ruefully. "It's a lot less expensive."

"According to my husband, American divorce records prove the impossibility."

"A remarkable fellow."

"Very."

The grass stalk was a mangled mess in his hands. He tossed it away and went to her swiftly and kissed her. Then he took her hand gently and led her through the creaking gateway of the shrine.

The grass was green and soft under the ancient olives, and from where they sat they could look through the bars of the gate and a broken section of the wall, to the fall of the hillside and the dazzle of the distant bay.

The air was drowsy with insects under the dappled leaves, and Cosima lay back on the warm grass and pillowed her head on her hands. Ashley sat beside her, hands clasped about his knees, abstracted and half afraid of the revelation he knew must soon come.

They tried to talk of old days in Rome. But the old days were like old kisses—cold and painful to remember. So they fell silent and let the warmth seep

38

into them, content with each other's presence, and the nostalgia of the lost paradise, half-bitter and half-sweet.

A long time later, Ashley looked down at her and said, quietly:

"Cosima, there's something to be said."

"Say it, Richard." Her voice was drowsy and contented.

"For the past six months I've been investigating your husband. I'm printing a story that may well ruin him. What you saw in the lounge today was part of it."

"I know, Richard."

"What?"

He sat bolt upright and looked down at her. She lay there placidly, smiling at him.

"I know, my dear. My husband knows too. That's why he's coming down today. That's why he sent Elena."

"Who is Elena?"

She pouted in amusement.

"His secretary—mistress, too, of course. Attractive, isn't she?"

"Yes, attractive."

He looked away from her, towards the crumbling wall and the small vista of sea and sky between the rusted bars of the gate. What did he say now? How did he frame a question that once asked might ruin everything—even the brief happiness of the last hour?

"I'll answer it for you, *caro mio*."

"Answer what?"

"The next question. Why did I come?"

"Well . . .?"

She sat up, put her arm around his shoulder and turned his face towards her.

"I came because my husband wished it. This is election time. There are appearances to be kept up. I came early because I knew you would be here and because I wanted this—this little time with you."

"Is that all?"

"Should there be any móre, Richard?"

"Only one thing. What do you want me to do about this story?"

"What do you want to do, *caro*?"

"Print it."

"Then print it, my dear. It doesn't worry me in the least."

Then she kissed him and drew him down to her on the warm and trampled grass. When the time came to go, he was happier than he had been for ten ambitious years.

The cicadas were silent and the first faint breeze was stirring in the grey leaves, as he backed the car out of the track and headed it down the long, winding road that led back to Sorrento. It was clear of traffic. The afternoon sight-seers were gone long since. Because they were late already, because he was relaxed and exhilarated, because there was strength in his hands and power under his feet, he drove fast and dangerously, rolling the long car round the curves, drifting it across the steep camber away from the high embankments.

He braked a little when they came to the last hair-pin bend and they turned on to a mile of straight road, banked high on one side and shaded with gnarled olives and, on the other, dropping away steeply towards the sea. He put his foot hard down on the accelerator and the Isotta leapt forward at full power, eating up the road.

Then Cosima screamed.

Directly ahead of them, there was a man standing and swaying dangerously on the edge of the embankment. Ashley trod on the brakes and swung out. As he did so the man seemed to leap out into mid-air, straight in front of the car. The tyres screamed and the wheels locked, but the momentum was too great and the fenders caught him and tossed him forward and they felt the bump as the car rode on top of him, rolling him over and over in the gravel like a limp rag doll.

Desperately, Ashley wrestled the car away from the edge of the drop and halted it fifty yards down the road. He got out, left Cosima slumped and sobbing in the seat, and went racing back towards the bloody bundle in the middle of the road.

When he turned it over, he saw that it was Enzo Garofano, the informer.

CHAPTER THREE

THE AIR WAS VERY STILL. Time itself was still. No bird sang, and the strident cicadas were dumb. The town in the valley was a painted town, the sea was a backcloth daub. The grey olives were nightmare trees. The sprawled shape in the middle of the road and the man who bent over him were puppet figures, motionless, waiting for the strings to jerk them into life.

Then the breeze stirred again. The leaves whispered and the branches creaked and Richard Ashley leaned forward over the body of Enzo Garofano.

He lay on his back, neck twisted and limbs spread at grotesque angles to his body. His chest was crushed. His face was torn and bloody and a dark pool of blood spread round him, soaking into the tattered dusty clothing. Twenty yards up the road his hat and his brief-case lay pitched against the side of the embankment.

The embankment. . . .

Ashley looked up. It was ten, twelve, feet high and the olives grew close to the edge, their branches overhanging the road. A minute ago, Garofano had stood there, swaying on the lip.

There was no footpath there. It was private property.

No place for a man to walk. The wall was grey tufa, scarred with the picks of the roadmakers, but sheer and steep. No place for a man to climb.

But Garofano had been neither walking nor climbing. He had been standing there, tottering as if . . . as if someone had thrust him towards the edge and sent him toppling and flailing in front of the speeding car.

Sick and shaking, Ashley straightened up and walked slowly up the road, to pick up the hat and the brief-case.

The hat was dusty and grease-stained. Mechanically he tried to clean it, rubbing it on his sleeve. The brief-case was intact, the zip-fastener was closed, but when he opened it, there was nothing inside. He looked up marking the spot from where Garofano had come. There was a huddle of small trees and one large fellow with a thick trunk and oddly twisted branches. The police would want to know that. The police would want to come and look for traces of the men who had killed this shabby little cheat with the narrow face and the furtive eyes.

Then it hit him.

The man who had killed Enzo Garofano was himself —Richard Ashley. He had threatened to do it, there were witnesses to prove that. He had done it, not three hours later. By misadventure truly, but there was only one witness to tell how it was done, and her testimony would be that of the biased lover and the faithless wife.

Or that of a conspirator, party to murder!

It was a horrifying thought, but it came to him with

brutal logic. Who else had known which way they would come? Who but she had chosen the way—'up the mountain, it's lonely there'. How, but from her, would they have known, the men who had brought Garofano to this spot and tossed him out into perdition?

But she had screamed in horror. Now she was huddled weeping in the car. She could not have expected this. But she didn't have to expect it. She had only to do as she was asked. Meet him, drive him up the mountain, keep him there a while. The rest was in other hands.

The motive? To protect her husband, to maintain the state and the fortune for which she had married him in the first place. But the prelude? The love under the olive trees, the rush of memories relived, the tenderness and the kisses? She had given him those too, in the old times—and then sold him out for Orgagna. If then, why not now, when the stakes were so much greater? Nothing so comforting as a title and a bank balance when autumn comes to the dark beauty of Rome.

Sudden nausea overcame him. His head spun and his face was clammy and he leaned his head against the grey stone of the embankment and retched painfully.

When the spasm had passed, he wiped his face and his hands, picked up the hat and the brief-case and walked back down the road towards the car. When he came abreast of the body, he stopped and looked down at it again. It was time to think of practical matters. He would have to get it into the car—Cosima's car—and

44

drive it to the Questura. He would have to make a report. They would be questioned, both of them. What story would they tell?

'. . . We are old lovers, you see. We went out to steal an hour under the olives of Il Deserto. I was crazy, as lovers are. I was driving fast. This fellow was thrown under the wheels of my car by friends of this lady's husband. . . . It is a fact that I threatened to kill him. It is a fact that I thrashed him in a public place . . . but this, this is something different—a snare, you understand. A trap for the unwary pedlar of the truth. . . .'

Even as he thought it, he knew it for a folly. The story they would tell must be different altogether. The truth, yes, because a lie would entangle them both when the real questioning began. But not the whole truth. And because they both must tell the same story, he must hide his suspicions of Cosima, must still play the lover and the protecting friend. Even, if possible, use her, as others had used her against him.

He had one strong card. Elections were coming up. It was necessary for Orgagna to keep up appearances. A scandal involving his wife and an old lover could do him much harm. If he were prepared to kill to save his name, he would certainly not jib at a convenient lie or two. Orgagna had influence in this country, where influence counted much more than integrity. It would be a sour irony to have him use it for the man who wanted to ruin him.

It was small hope, but it gave him courage to walk

45

back and comfort Cosima, then to back the car up and bundle the limp, heavy bundle into the back seat, lay the brief-case on its chest and cover its face with the hat, so that it might ride back to Sorrento with decency.

Then, very carefully, he explained matters to Cosima. She was white and trembling, her face was ravaged with shocked weeping and she sat away from him in the corner of the seat, eyes carefully averted from the grim burden in the back. But she listened attentively and seemed to understand what he wanted her to do.

". . . We drive back to town. I'll put the hood up and the side-screens. First, I'll go to the hotel and leave you there. Then I'll drive round to the Questura, deliver the car and the body and make my report."

"But—but the police will want to see both of us."

"Sure. But the police are gentlemen. They will understand that the Duchess of Orgagna is a delicate lady and deeply shocked. They will make their enquiries later, when Her Excellency is rested and has the support of her husband."

"What will you tell them?"

"The truth. We were driving fast. No point in denying that. The skidmarks and the state of the body are clear evidence. My excuse is that you had a dinner date, which is true. And the road was empty, which is also true. I'll explain how we saw Garofano on top of the embankment; how he seemed to fall right in front of the car; how we picked him up and brought him down

46

to the town. That's all—no explanations, nothing."

"How do you explain—us?"

"We are old friends. Your husband and I have met. You wanted to show me the beauties of the hill drive. It's the truth—part of it at least—and it involves us in no lies. Do you understand that? We mustn't lie. We mustn't embellish. If we do, we're in difficulties, both of us."

"I—I understand."

"The point is, will your husband understand? Will he support your story? And claim me as an old acquaintance entitled to the courtesy of your company?"

She smiled at him then, wanly.

"He hasn't much choice, has he?"

"None at all," said Ashley grimly. He switched on the ignition and started the engine. Cosima laid a detaining hand on his arm.

"Richard, there's one thing. . . ."

"Yes?"

"How do you explain it to the police?"

"Explain what?"

She gestured vaguely at the embankment.

"How he came to be up there—how he fell. I mean it sounds so silly and unreal. The sort of thing that makes us both look ridiculous, as if we're inventing a story to excuse our speeding."

"Look, sweetheart!" He turned to her and laid it down bluntly. "We tell it that way because, however it sounds, it's the truth."

She shook her head wearily.

"You don't understand Neapolitans. You certainly don't understand the Neapolitan police. Give them half a line of drama, they want to turn it into an opera. What is true is not so important as what looks true. It makes it easier for the police, and it makes it easier for us. You have to help them to a convenient way out. A simple accident with no complications, nothing for the journalists to make into a story."

"What do you want me to tell them, Cosima?"

"Why, simply that . . . that this man was walking up the hill with his eyes on the road. You saw him too late. You sounded your horn. He jumped the wrong way and you hit him. A simple story that worries no one and no one can disprove. An accident, you see?"

"No," said Ashley flatly, "I don't."

"But, Richard. . . ."

"We tell it the way it happened." His eyes were hard. His mouth was tight as a trap.

"You don't understand. You don't know the way things work here."

He didn't bother to reply. He revved the engine and eased the Isotta out into the middle of the road. He understood all too well. To kill a pedestrian on a mile of empty road is culpable homicide in any codex. Given the motive, you can make it look like wilful murder. He knew now, for certain, that Cosima had betrayed him.

48

Slowly, very slowly, he drove down the winding, mountain road.

Captain Eduardo Granforte was a large soft man with tiny hands and feet. He had a round, innocent face, a velvet voice, an oblique smile and gentle eyes. He liked his job, because it was easy. He wanted it kept that way. He was a courteous fellow, who understood how to deal with foreign visitors and particularly with representatives of the foreign press. He helped Ashley over the first rough passages with a speed and efficiency that left him gasping.

The Isotta was whisked swiftly away from public view, to be washed and cleaned. The body of Garofano was deposited in a spare cell of the prison to await an autopsy. A telephone call to the hotel brought clean clothes for Ashley, whose shirt and trousers were bloody from his handling of the body. Coffee was brought and American cigarettes and the questioning proceeded with an unexpected charm.

". . . The car, you say, is the property of Her Excellency the Duchess of Orgagna?"

"That's right."

"She had asked you to drive it?"

"Yes."

"You have an international licence?"

"Yes. I wasn't carrying it, but . . ."

Captain Granforte smiled gently and waved a deprecating hand.

49

"Enough that you possess it, *signore*. We do not stand on minor ceremonies—unless we have to, of course."

"You're very kind."

"*Prego, signore!*" The Captain bowed to the compliment. "Now, you went out for your drive. You were returning in a hurry as Her Excellency had a dinner engagement."

"Yes."

"What was your speed at the time of the accident?" Ashley shrugged:

"I couldn't say. I hadn't looked at the meter. It was quite fast."

"But, there are so many curves on the road, it could not have been excessively so."

Ashley was quick to seize the line that was flung to him. The Captain was playing it carefully. Orgagna was a big fellow. The sort of fellow who could do much for a provincial police captain—provided he knew how to behave himself.

"No, that's true—the curves do slow you down."

"So, you are proceeding at reasonable speed along this stretch of the road. What then?"

"Her Excellency screamed. It startled me because the road was clear. I looked up and saw a man right on the edge of the high embankment. He was swaying. I swung out. The next minute he—he seemed to leap out into the air, right in front of the car. I braked, but the fender hit him and we went over him. I stopped the car, ran back, found he was dead. Then I backed up, loaded him into the car and brought him here. And— and that's all."

The Captain frowned. His gentle eyes clouded. His soft fingers drummed on the desk. The smooth stream of his questions was checked. He looked thoughtfully up at the ceiling. Then he put it to Ashley.

"The circumstances, as you describe them, are rather unusual."

"Yes."

The Captain looked at him sharply.

"Did you think so at the time?"

"At the time, no. I was trying to control the car. I had no time to think of anything else."

"But afterwards?"

"Afterwards when I went back, I looked up the embankment. I saw that it was private property. There was no footpath. There was no way to climb up there. I wondered about how he got there and what he was doing so close to the edge and how he came to fall."

"Did any answers suggest themselves to you?"

Ashley shrugged wearily. His head was buzzing. He was beginning to feel the effects of delayed shock.

"None. Besides, I had other things to think about. Garofano was dead. My guesswork wouldn't help him any."

"Garofano?" The Captain pounced on the word like

a cat. "You know the man then? You have heard his name?"

Ashley put his hands on the edge of the desk to stop their sudden trembling. It was his first mistake; but it was too late to mend it now. He tried to make his answer sound indifferent.

"I know him. I've done business with him."

"What sort of business."

"He used to sell me occasional news items."

"When did you last see him? Before the accident?"

"Four-thirty this afternoon at the Caravino."

"Shortly before you left for your drive with Her Excellency?"

"That's right."

Captain Granforte looked at his wrist-watch. A quarter to eight. Too close to dinner-time. Too late for any man to be working. He had many more questions to ask this leather-faced American, but now was not the time to ask them. It seemed to him that there were other things to be inquired into first: the involvement of the Duchess of Orgagna and of her husband; the status of the American in that curious domestic arrangement; the background of Garofano; the nature of the information he had been peddling to a foreign correspondent; how he had come to be at the top of the embankment; how he had come to fall. Any one of these questions seemed likely to lead him into troubled waters. He preferred to make his own soundings before venturing out any further. There might be shoals and quicksands for an ambitious official with his way to make in the world.

He leaned his chin on his small feminine hands and smiled genially at Ashley across the desk.

"You've had a bad afternoon, my friend."

"Very."

"You will, of course, be staying in Sorrento for a few days."

"Yes."

"You are not likely to leave without informing us first?"

"No."

"Then permit me to offer you a cognac before we both have dinner."

"Thanks. I could use a drink."

They stood up together. In the shabby, fly-spotted room of the Questura, Richard Ashley drank cognac with the man who might soon put a noose around his neck. Captain Eduardo Granforte smiled and smiled and talked about women. It was a subject he enjoyed immensely.

Twenty minutes later Ashley walked back into the Hotel Caravino. He stopped at the desk to pick up his key and take the manuscript out of safe-deposit and order a bottle of whisky to be sent to his room. The clerk looked at him oddly, but said nothing. On his way to the lift, he glanced in at the bar. There was the usual clutter of pre-dinner drinkers, but in one corner he saw Elena Carrese deep in conversation with a slim, smooth-cheeked youth in a sharkskin jacket. There was no sign of Cosima.

The lift came down, disgorged a small gaggle of women in backless frocks and men in tropical mess-jackets. They made him feel shabby and crumpled.

As he rode up to the third floor, he wondered if he should try to telephone Cosima, to tell her the result of his interview with the police. He decided against it. Safer to leave the next move to her. On the day's showing, she had more talent for intrigue than he could muster.

Arrived at his room, he ran a deep, steaming bath, stripped and lowered himself into it. His whole body ached as if he had been beaten with rods. Slowly, the warmth relaxed him, the tension slacked off and he lay, stretched in the tub, making the tally of his fortieth birthday.

It was all a dead loss.

His big story was wrecked, because Garofano had cheated him of the Orgagna photostats. The woman he loved had betrayed him and walked him, smiling, into a snare. He had killed a man by driving like a drunken idiot. Any time from now he might face an indictment under Italian law for manslaughter, even for murder.

The tale of the accident would be buzzing about the town. The tale of his quarrel with Garofano was already gossip in the servants' quarters. All too soon the story would come to the ears of the moon-faced Captain. Then the game would start in earnest.

Arrest, imprisonment perhaps. In Italian law the driver is guilty by presumption. The slow, subtle processes of Italian law . . . They would drag the case on and on until after the elections, before releasing him on an equivocal verdict. By that time Orgagna would have his seat in the Cabinet and the Office would have a polite request from the American Embassy to transfer him out of Italy as *persona non grata*.

It was neat and dramatically effective. And the man who had stage-managed the comedy was Vittorio, Duke of Orgagna.

When he thought about Orgagna, he could not grudge him respect, even reluctant admiration. It takes a very particular kind of courage to watch a man month after month piling up evidence for your damnation and yet to do nothing about it. It takes a gambler's nerve to feed line after line of evidence to your prosecutor, and then dangle the final documents in front of him, so that when he stretches for them he may over-reach and topple himself into ruin.

Orgagna had done just that. But there was more to it than nerve and courage. There was subtlety and skill— a thousand years of diplomacy and intrigue. He had moved his pieces through strategy after strategy until he had stripped the board and left his opponent checkmated, ringed about by the minions of the black king—

55   c

Cosima, Elena Carrese, George Harlequin, Captain Granforte.

Even for the victim, there was a sour satisfaction in so much technical brilliance.

Ashley hoisted himself out of the bath, towelled himself and shaved carefully. He dressed with more than usual care and spent minutes over the set of his dinner bow. As he fiddled with it, he grinned unhappily at the mirror. A man who is going to his own funeral likes to make it a dressy occasion.

There was a knock at the door. Ashley called, "*Avanti!*" and a waiter came in with whisky and glasses and a silver bucket of ice. Ashley signed the chit, gave the waiter a hundred lire and ushered him out of the door. Then he poured himself a two-finger measure, watered it and sat himself in the arm-chair by the terrace window to take another look at his problem.

The telephone jangled at his elbow. He lifted the receiver and said, carefully:

"*Pronto!* This is Richard Ashley."

"Richard?" It was Cosima's voice, careful, controlled, neutral. "This is Cosima. How did you get on at the Questura?"

"Very well, so far. I made my report. The Captain may wish to see me again. That's all."

"Good!" She said it with cool courtesy. "I'm very glad. Er, Richard?"

"Yes?"

"My husband is very grateful for your courtesy in

56

handling this part of the business. He'd like you to join us for dinner in our suite."

"The hell he would!" said Ashley in blank amazement.

"I'm so glad," said Cosima, politely. "Shall we say in twenty minutes?"

"Oh—sure . . . sure,"

"Then we can both thank you together. *Arrivederci!*"

The line went dead and Ashley sat staring stupidly into the mouthpiece of the phone. Then he laid it carefully on the cradle, stood up, walked out on the balcony and looked out over the moonlit water.

The sea was calm. The night was warm and windless, but he shivered as if someone had walked over his grave. He wasn't dead yet, of course, but the gravediggers had started work.

Thinking of death, he thought also of Enzo Garofano, who was dead today and tomorrow would be buried and forgotten. He was a frightened, furtive fellow out for a quick profit. Yet he might have toppled a government and set the chancelleries of Europe buzzing like smoked bees, because somehow he had come to possess six photostat copies of private letters written by Orgagna to business colleagues and political connections.

How had he come by them? It was a question Ashley had asked him at their first meeting, but he had sidestepped it. He had connections, he said—connections in the household of the great man. Through these con-

57

nections he had been able to take the original letters into his possession, display them to Ashley, photograph them and return them to Orgagna's files. Ashley had accepted the explanation as the only one possible. He had been less interested in the circumstances than in the documents themselves, which proved conclusively the negotiation of a government loan of two million dollars to establish a textile industry in the South and the fraudulent diversion of ninety per cent of the funds to Orgagna enterprises in the North.

Now the circumstances themselves were of vital importance. Garofano had contacted him in Naples and arranged a meeting at Sorrento. He had presented the originals of the letters for inspection. It seemed unlikely that these had come from Rome. More likely they had come from the files in the summer villa. The contact, therefore, belonged to the Sorrento household, or at least had access to it.

What then was the basis of the collusion between this unnamed contact and Enzo Garofano? If the contact were a man, the motive was profit. If a woman, profit, too, perhaps, but other things as well ... love, jealousy, revenge. But with Garofano dead, there could be no profit, therefore ...

'. . . Therefore find your contact, Richard Ashley, and you may be able to resume business. There are two thousand dollars in bright American notes waiting at American Express. It's a bait, even for big fish, so long as you dangle it in the right pool.'

He looked out across the placid water to the clustered lights of the fishing-boats and puzzled over a new question. Why was he doing it? Why at forty years of age was he still involved in this shabby business of intrigue and subornation in the name of news? The romantics glorified it as a noble profession. The cynics damned it as sordid speculation on the miseries of the world. The idealists claimed to be apostles. The hucksters profited from the prurient curiosity of millions. Yet, monitor or muck-raker, the journalist had at his disposal a channel of communication, through which, pure or polluted, the truth trickled each day to millions of people all over the world.

It wasn't the whole truth. It never could be. But even part of the truth was better than the conspiracy of silence in which corruption flourished like a rank growth.

But it took more than the truth to keep a man twenty years in the same bed, to keep him curious and passionate, and ambitious for renewed conquest.

His vanity must be fed with banner-lines and by-lines and special assignments. His pride must be fed with the greatest illusion of all—that the man who reports the news is the man who makes it. His sensuality must be soothed with doses of easy living among the people whose lives he observes but never truly shares. And, more than all else, you must give him a goal—the big story! As though the fall of a government and the re-shuffle of office and perquisites were more important in the human scale than the birth of a mewing child or the dying prayer of an old, old man.

It was a comfortless thought and he put it away from him. He was forty years of age, committed long since to the pursuit of the bright illusion. He was too old to turn back. He must walk to the end of the road. He must reach up for the dangling fruit, though he knew it would be, like the apples of Sodom, a dry dust in his mouth.

He looked at his watch. It still lacked ten minutes to dinner-time. Time for another drink—one for the crooked road.

CHAPTER FOUR

ORGAGNA'S DINNER PARTY was as intimate as a press reception, and as carefully staged.

When Ashley knocked at the door of the suite, it was opened by a steward in a white coat, who led him into a room half as large as a ballroom, with a winking chandelier and a great view window that looked out over the bay towards the lights of Naples and the flaring beacons of the gas-plants near Pugliano.

A long table was laid under the window and a *maître d'hôtel* in a frock-coat was fussing over two waiters and a shining array of hot plates. Orgagna was there and Harlequin and the blonde secretary, whose name was Elena, and the epicene young escort he had seen in the lounge bar. Cosima was there, too, and she came forward to greet him—not the wind-blown beauty of the afternoon's adventure, but the hostess of a ducal *salon*, her body sheathed in gold, her face a smiling mask, her eyes a blank mockery.

"My dear Richard! Kind of you to come."

"A pleasure, Cosima."

He took her hand and bent over it, continental fashion, brushing it lightly with his lips, feeling it lie, slack and unresponsive in his palm. Then Orgagna came forward, tall, aquiline, ironic eyes and grey hair and the practised charm of the diplomat.

"Mr. Ashley! We have met before, I think—professionally. I'm glad you were able to come. You have put me in your debt."

"Your Excellency exaggerates," said Ashley coolly. If they wanted it played this way, a comedy of old-world manners, he was willing to oblige.

Orgagna took his arm and led him on the ritual circuit of the guests.

"Harlequin you've already met, I believe."

"Several times."

George Harlequin looked at him with pale and speculative eyes.

"Sorry to hear of your accident, Ashley."

"One of those things." Ashley shrugged indifferently and allowed himself to be led towards Elena Carrese and the tall, willowy youth who stood beside her. The first sight of her shocked him. The air of vacuous charm was gone. Her eyes were hostile. Even the careful make-up could not conceal the fact that she had been weeping. The hand that held the glass was trembling and the liquor canted perilously towards the brim. Orgagna skated quickly through the introductions.

"My secretary, Elena Carrese."

"*Signorina*."

"Tullio Riccioli, one of the most promising young artists in Rome."

"*Signore.*"

The young man offered him a soft hand and a vague greeting and turned back to Elena Carrese. Orgagna steered his guest back to Cosima and Harlequin. A waiter brought him a champagne cocktail and they stood together, working their way through the intricate maze of polite conversation towards the subject that concerned them all.

Ashley began with a bald statement of fact.

"I've brought the car back. The police were kind enough to have it washed. The keys are at the desk."

"You have been very thoughtful, Mr. Ashley," said Orgagna warmly. "To spare my wife the trouble of an interview with the police was a charity not easily forgotten. She was badly shocked when she arrived here, but she is better now, aren't you, *cara*?"

Cosima turned on her bright empty smile.

"Much better. Did—did you have any trouble, Richard?"

"No. The Captain was very considerate."

"He accepted your explanation of the accident?" It was Orgagna's question, pointed but unanxious.

"He accepted it, yes. I'm not sure that he believed it."

"What gave you that impression?" There was an edge to Orgagna's voice and his eyes were bright with interest.

Cosima said nothing, but watched them both tensely. George Harlequin listened with polite detachment.

63

Ashley's answer was blunt. His patience had worn thin.

"He seemed to find something sinister in my story of a man toppling from the embankment. I gathered that he would like to make other inquiries. He made it clear that I was to stay in Sorrento."

"Will—will he want to see me, Richard?"

"Probably."

Orgagna dismissed the idea, cheerfully.

"What does it matter, *cara*? He will want to see you, certainly. It is the routine. You give him the facts. He goes away and makes twenty copies for all the bureaucrats who are concerned in the matter. It is his job, you should not let it interfere with your digestion."

"Foolish of me, of course." Cosima smiled uneasily and sipped her cocktail.

Orgagna offered Ashley a cigarette. Harlequin lit it for him. His pale eyes were full of questions, but the one he asked was the shrewdest of all.

"Do *you* think there was anything sinister in the business, Ashley?"

It took him a shade off-balance, but he recovered quickly. He damned the canny little agent to hell and back, but he forced a grin and shrugged off the inquiry.

"The facts are more than enough for me just now. I'll leave speculation to the experts."

"Wise fellow," said George Harlequin mildly.

"To a man in a new country," said Orgagna smoothly, "everything is strange and sometimes sinister. The first time I went to London, I was oppressed by the tolling of Big Ben. He sounded to me like the Miserere bell. It took me a long time to understand that he was a friendly fellow beloved by his people. It is the same with Mr. Ashley. He has had an unnerving experience. He cannot regard it as a normal accident. The image is still vivid and of nightmare quality."

"We're discussing the Captain's views, not mine." Ashley was tiring of diplomatic subtleties. The calculating selfishness of these people shocked him. A man was dead—an insignificant unlovely fellow, surely, but a man still, with a body and a soul, born of woman, loved perhaps by woman, father of sons, maybe. One of these folk had plotted his murder, the others were joined to the act by tacit approbation. Yet they stood there, smiling, gesturing like actors on a set, probing for information to comfort them in their uneasiness. He wanted to damn them to the devil and leave them. But he, too, had need of information, so he stood there, playing out the sardonic comedy, studying their smooth well-bred faces for signs and portents. It was Cosima who gave him the first, small lead. She faced him squarely and said:

"I warned you, didn't I, Richard? Give a Neapolitan a hint of drama and he will blow it up into a theatre piece. You would have been better advised to make the thing simple. The man was walking along the road. You sounded your horn and tried to swerve. He moved the wrong way. . . . Simple, straightforward."

"Too simple, Cosima."

"Why, Richard?"

Why? The truth was trembling on his tongue: 'Because it sets me up for a murder charge and leaves your precious husband scot-free. Because my only hope—and it's a slim one—is to have Captain Granforte examine the ground at the top of the embankment for signs of a struggle. Because . . .' But he didn't say it. Instead, he explained patiently:

"In any country to kill a man on a mile of open road points to dangerous driving. That's a serious charge. The charge in Italy could be more serious still—culpable homicide. Better for both of us," he leaned a little on the phrase, "—better for both of us if we can avoid that one."

A flicker of interest showed in Harlequin's pale eyes. Orgagna looked thoughtful, then nodded, sagely.

"Mr. Ashley is right, of course, Cosima. In any case it is wiser not to tamper with the truth, even for the sake of convenience."

"Much wiser," said Richard Ashley.

There was a pause, as if a little chill wind had blown through the room, stirring the smooth surface of the talk, ruffling up the weedy tangle of motives and counter-motives that lay beneath it.

Then, once more, Orgagna took command of the situation. He signalled to the *maître d'hôtel*, and the party was swept instantly into the sedulous flurry of

66

dinner-service. The waiters settled them into their chairs—Orgagna at the head, Cosima at the foot of the table, Ashley and Harlequin side by side facing Elena Carrese and the young artist, who sat with their backs to the window.

The wine was poured and the food was brought and they might have been any party of wealthy internationals met for enjoyment in the Siren Land. Harlequin began a three-cornered conversation with Tullio and Orgagna on Roman exhibitions and trends in modern Italian painting. Ashley was left with the thankless job of entertaining an old mistress and the woman who had supplanted her in her husband's bed.

He was less than successful. Elena's replies to his first gambits were brusque and sullen. Cosima battled vainly to maintain the air of bright detachment proper to a virtuous wife. Before they were half-way through the fish, the conversation was dead and they sat listening to the animated discussion at the head of the table. Ashley was glad of the relief. It left him free to think. And his first thoughts were of the blonde girl with the strained, unhappy face who sat opposite him.

The change in her was startling. Her mannequin charm was gone, stripped off like a carnival mask. Her face was tight and strange. Her empty, laughing eyes were full now of brooding hate. Why? Because he had driven out with the wife of her lover? That might be matter for laughter or triumph, but not for tears.

Because he had killed a man? But what connection could there be between a shabby little huckster like Garofano and this expensive secretary-mistress from the *salons* of Rome?

How else explain the sudden change from impersonal flirtation to lively hate? Unless Orgagna had sensed her possible interest in him and had made some new malice to set her against him. It was possible. Anything was possible at this stagey dinner party.

". . . don't you agree, Mr. Ashley?" Orgagna's voice started him out of his reverie.

"I'm sorry, I didn't catch the question."

"We were talking of morals—the morals of art and the morals of politics."

Ashley shrugged.

"I'm a newsman, not a philosopher."

"Come, come, my dear fellow!" Orgagna rallied him with apparent good-humour. "That is the function of the press, is it not? The whole justification of the Fourth Estate is that it should be a monitor of public morals."

Anger soured the taste of the wine. They were at him again, pricking and goading, watching his reaction to each new pique. But anger was what they wanted—anger and indiscretion. He dared not yield to them. He sipped his wine and framed his answer, carefully.

"Tonight is a privileged occasion, Your Excellency. It would be bad manners to discuss the morals of the press—or of the politicians."

George Harlequin laughed suddenly and choked over his wine.

"Privileged occasion! That's very good indeed. Odd you know, Orgagna, we never expect the Americans to be phrase-makers. Ashley here is quite an adept."

"I have never underrated Mr. Ashley's talents," said Orgagna, with thin urbanity. "I am glad he is our friend and not an enemy."

'Now,' thought Ashley, 'now we come to the core of the apple. He wants a truce. He knows he can embarrass me—he is not sure I can be silenced. He wants to make a bargain. A little more patience and he will lay down the terms of it.'

The thought cheered him. He acknowledged the compliment with a grin and the tension slacked off. Cosima made a remark about fashions. Harlequin capped it. The slim youth joined in with eager feminine interest and the awkward moment passed. Only Elena Carrese sat sullen and silent, with a moonlit sea and the lights of the distant city a background for her sombre beauty.

The plates were changed and the new wine was broken out. The waiters hovered attentively as the *signori* ate and talked of high fashion and high finance, of society scandals and curial intrigues. Their faces were blank, their eyes expressionless, as befits good servants. But their ears were open and attentive, storing up the scraps of gossip and the tag-ends of information. In the breadline economies of the South, a well-timed tip might mean an extra kilo of *pasta* on the family table or a warm coat for an ailing child.

The roast was served and the highly-coloured pastries. The fruit was brought and the cheeses. The strong, bitter coffee was expressed in the silver percolator and the *maître d'hôtel* was warming the big balloons for the brandy when, sharp and strident, the telephone rang.

The *maître d'hôtel* laid down the brandy-bubble and went to answer it. His voice was low and noncommittal; he cast a quick shrewd glance at the company round the table, then laid down the receiver and hurried over to Orgagna. He bent close to him and whispered in his ear. Orgagna listened attentively, then excused himself and went into the bedroom to take the call on another phone.

Cosima watched him go with troubled, inquiring eyes.

Three minutes later he was back. He made no reference to the call but picked up the conversation where he had left off.

Then, when the coffee was served and the brandy, he turned to the *maître d'hôtel*.

"You may leave us now. If we need anything we shall ring."

"Yes, Excellency."

He bowed and left the room, flapping the waiters before him like a mother hen with a pair of chickens. Orgagna sat relaxed in his chair staring down at the brandy bowl between his cupped hands. Without looking up, he said coolly:

"Tullio, take Elena down to the lounge and give her coffee and brandy there. Don't leave the hotel. I may need you both later."

Without a word, the young man and the girl stood up and left the room. Orgagna waited until the door closed behind them. Then he looked up. His eyes were cold. His mouth was grim. The others watched him, puzzled and uneasy. Then he spoke:

"That phone call was from Captain Granforte at the Questura. He wished to interview you, Mr. Ashley."

"He hasn't wasted much time."

Orgagna waved aside the interruption.

"I pointed out to the Captain that, because of my wife, I, too, was involved in this matter. I have asked him, as a favour, to join us here, where we may discuss in privacy whatever problems are involved. He has consented to do that."

"Kind of him," said Ashley dryly.

"Kinder than you know, Mr. Ashley." Orgagna looked up, sharply. "We would be wise to use these few minutes to prepare ourselves for the discussion."

"I'm willing to listen."

"Good." Orgagna sipped his brandy, savouring the rich spirit deliberately. Then he set down his glass and leaned forward. His long, expressive hands emphasised each careful phrase. "I'm not unaware, Ashley, of your former relationship with my wife. Privately I have chosen to ignore it. Publicly I must suppress it, at all costs. For this reason, I am prepared to subscribe to a fiction—that you are my friend, that your drive this afternoon was a favour to me and a pleasant politeness to Cosima."

"I think that's a wise decision," said Ashley coolly.

Orgagna took another careful sip of brandy.

"Granforte is, apparently, aware of a—a business relationship between yourself and the man you killed. For this reason he finds certain sinister aspects in the accident. I imagine . . ." Orgagna looked down at the table and paused a moment. "—I am, of course, only guessing—that he will wish to bring charges of sufficient gravity to hold you here, pending a further investigation."

"Which could be embarrassing to you?"

"Because of my wife, yes."

"Have it your own way."

Orgagna ignored the irony and went on, choosing his words with nice deliberation.

"Therefore, our interests are identical. There would seem to be grounds for an alliance."

"What's the price?" asked Ashley bluntly.

"The price we can discuss later, if you survive this interview with Captain Granforte."

"If we both survive it."

Orgagna pushed his chair back from the table and stood up. His tone was indifferent.

"Later, perhaps, we may debate the issue. Think it

72

over, Mr. Ashley. We haven't much time. Come, Cosima."

He moved to the far end of the table, helped Cosima from her chair, and together they walked into the bedroom. The door closed behind them and Ashley was left alone with George Harlequin.

Imperturbable as ever, the little man sipped his brandy. His pale eyes were lit with malicious amusement. Ashley lit a cigarette and waited.

"I warned you, didn't I?"

Ashley looked at him with cold contempt.

"I've seen some dirty things done in the name of Her Majesty's Government, Harlequin. I didn't expect murder."

"Murder?" The smile was quenched in the pale eyes. They were lifeless as pebbles in the smooth boyish face.

"Orgagna arranged it, with his wife as an accessory and me as executioner."

"I don't believe it."

"Naturally." Ashley was weary now. His patience was stretched to breaking point. He was sick of them all—sick of their devious speech and their subtle contriving. But he was caught in the net they had spread for him and he could no more be quit of them than he could of himself or the ambition that drove him. The big story had blown up in his face, but the wreckage was piled on top of him, pinning him down.

Cold and aloof, George Harlequin watched him. He studied the lean brown face and the strong, nervous hands on the white napery. He, too, was limed and caught and, in a franker moment, he might have admitted it. But now, in this moment, in this room, sitting over the wreckage of the ducal dinner, he was a professional committed to all the sordid shifts of his trade. His flat precise voice was wintry as he laid down the next statement:

"Orgagna knows you've got the photostats."

"What?" Ashley started up as if he had been stuck with a pin. "Say that again!"

"Orgagna knows you've got the photostats."

Ashley looked at him a moment, gaping in wonderment. Then he threw back his head and laughed and laughed. Orgagna and Cosima hurried out of the bedroom and the three of them stood watching him, listening to his wild, hysterical mirth that bounced and echoed round the walls of the room and up among the plaster cupids on the ceiling.

Two minutes later Captain Granforte arrived and there was no laughter left in him.

CHAPTER FIVE

CAPTAIN EDUARDO GRANFORTE was a singularly happy man. He sat at ease in the *salon* of His Excellency, the Duke of Orgagna, with a fine brandy cradled in his soft hands and a tabular list of profitable information tucked away in his brain-box.

The information gave him confidence, but he was too experienced to fall into arrogance. He was sure of a minimum profit, but he knew that with tact and discretion he might increase it considerably.

He was not a corrupt man, though he served a corrupt administration. He was honest with himself—which is the greatest honesty of all—and he knew that while all men had a price, Granforte's price was probably higher than most. He had never perverted justice, though he had often connived at injustice when it was too strong for the creaky machinery of the Italian legal system. He had never taken a bribe, but he saw no point in refusing an honorarium from a grateful citizen.

So now, as he sat at the centre of the little arc of people, Orgagna, Cosima, Harlequin and Richard Ashley, he was pervaded with well-being and his interrogation was deceptively humble.

"We accept, Mr. Ashley, the fact of your long friendship with their Excellencies." He bowed towards the pair of them. "This explains, more than satisfactorily, your presence on the road at this hour, the use of a car which is not your own, even, possibly, a certain *brio* in your driving."

"A pleasant way to put it," said Ashley tersely.

"However," Granforte gestured widely with his glass, "we are less happy with reports of your own relations with the dead man."

"Why?"

"First, we understand that you were doing business with him."

"I've already told you that."

"What sort of business?"

"I've told you that, too. Buying information."

"What sort of information?"

"News items."

"Could you be more specific, Mr. Ashley?"

"No."

"Why not?"

"It is part of the ethics of my profession, Captain."

Captain Granforte smiled pleasantly. He didn't need the information. He had it all listed in his very capacious brain-box. It amused him to tease this big, confident American. It profited him to impress the dark-faced Duke and his beautiful and faithless wife. The more they respected him, the more they would be prepared to concede, when the time came to strike a bargain. He questioned Ashley again:

"It would, therefore, be true to say that the information you were buying from Garofano was of a confidential nature?"

"That's right."

"What do you know about Enzo Garofano, Mr. Ashley?"

"Nothing. He approached me with an offer of information. I checked the facts and not the man. The facts were sound. I was prepared to buy. I didn't care to know any more about him."

"Then permit me to tell you, Mr. Ashley. Garofano is—or was—a clerk in the Municipio of Naples."

"Interesting."

"More than interesting, Mr. Ashley, relevant. Your actions lay you open to a charge of suborning a public official to gain access to Government information."

Ashley shook his head and smiled grimly.

"You'll have to do better than that, Captain. The information had nothing to do with Government files. Even if it had, you couldn't prove it. Try again."

"Do you deny, Mr. Ashley," Granforte stabbed at him with a plump finger, "do you deny that the information was in the form of documents?"

"No, I don't deny that."

"Would you be good enough to show me the documents?"

"I don't have them."

"Why not?"

77

"Garofano wanted too much for them. I refused to buy."

"And then, Mr. Ashley," the Captain's voice was smooth as silk, "and then you quarrelled with this man in the lounge of the hotel. You struck him several times. You were heard to threaten his life."

"By whom?"

"By the barman, Roberto. Do you deny that?"

"No. It's quite true."

"*Allora!*" Captain Granforte leaned back in his chair and sniffed the last fading bouquet of the brandy. "You see the point to which we are arrived, Mr. Ashley. You make a public display of violence. You utter a public threat. You admit a motive—the refusal to sell certain documents. An hour later you run this man down on a straight stretch of open road. You bring him in to me. You bring also his brief-case, which is empty. You see the inference?"

"A moment, Captain!" It was Orgagna who spoke. He was leaning forward in his chair, tense, strained.

The Captain held up a deprecating hand.

"Please, Your Excellency, allow me to finish. I know what you are going to say. To make an accusation of this kind is to join Your Excellency's wife to a pre-meditated crime. This is, of course, unthinkable."

"Thank you, Captain," said Orgagna softly. He sat back slowly in his chair, watching Granforte from under hooded lids.

"Therefore, it is necessary to examine in more detail

the events of the afternoon, the movements of Mr. Ashley and of your wife, the movements of Garofano after he left the hotel, to show clearly the accidental nature of his death. On the other hand——"

Ashley stiffened and waited for it. The soft-faced Captain was no fool. In his own circuitous fashion he was walking towards the truth.

"—there may be information which Mr. Ashley has so far failed to put into our hands."

"I have nothing more to tell you, Captain."

Granforte pursed his full red lips and cocked his head on one side.

"Have you any suggestions which might help us in this investigation?"

"Yes."

"What are they, Mr. Ashley?"

"Send your men out to look at the top of the embankment where Garofano fell. It may give you some idea of how he came to be there and what caused him to fall."

The Captain nodded.

"We have already thought of that, Mr. Ashley. Unfortunately there is nothing we can do till the daylight. It is my own view that we shall find nothing, but I am prepared to keep an open mind."

He might have said much more.

He might have said that there were two policemen cursing the night away under the olive trees, with orders to arrest anyone who came near the spot. He might have said that he had checked the survey of the Commune and found that the place from which Garofano had fallen was the boundary of the Orgagna estates.

But he was a shrewd fellow who liked to keep a shot or two in reserve. He sat back in his chair, moon-faced and genial, and waited for someone to ask him a question. He was surprised when it came from George Harlequin.

"Where did this fellow live . . . this Garofano?"

"In Sant'Agata, on top of the hill."

"The assumption would be, therefore, that, after he left the hotel, he would be going home?"

"Probably."

"Would he go on foot? It's a long way."

"Normally one would expect him to take the bus. But leaving the hotel at the time he did, he would have missed it. The next one would not leave for two hours. He may have chosen to walk."

"And he would necessarily have taken the same road as Mr. Ashley and Her Excellency?"

"It is the only road, *signore*."

"It is possible, therefore, that other people who were interested in his movements could have followed him without difficulty."

"What other people?"

Harlequin shrugged.

"I couldn't begin to guess. But it seems reasonable to me that if he refused to sell the information or the documents to Mr. Ashley, it would be because he had another buyer."

The Captain turned a questioning eye on Ashley.

"It might help us to establish that point if Mr. Ashley would give us some idea of the nature of the documents."

For a long moment Ashley considered the proposition. At first sight it was tempting. It shifted the guilt and the onus of disproof on to the shoulders of Orgagna. It left him free to continue his search for the photostats. It put the big story once more within the limits of possibility. But it left too much to chance: the influence of Orgagna, the attitude of Cosima, who thus far had not even been questioned, the attitude of Harlequin himself, who was too seasoned a negotiator to hand so obvious an advantage to his opponent. He felt suddenly small and lonely, naked to the daggers of intrigue in an old and alien country. He shook his head.

"I'm sorry. I have nothing more to say."

He heard the long, soft exhalation of Orgagna's breath. He saw Cosima's tense hands relax in her lap. He caught Harlequin's little gesture of indifferent dismissal. He watched Captain Granforte finish the last of his brandy and reach into his breast pocket for a cigarette-case. He wondered what was going on behind those genial eyes and that round sallow face. He had not long to wait.

Granforte took the cigarette-case out of his pocket, held it between thumb and forefinger and beat a little tattoo on the arm of the chair. Then he looked at Ashley.

"In that case, Mr. Ashley, I have no alternative but to place you under arrest on charges of subornation of officials and culpable homicide. More serious charges may be preferred later as the result of our investigations."

Ashley was suddenly calm. He stood up.

"You must do your duty as you see it, Captain. I must ask you, however, to telephone immediately to the American Consul in Naples and arrange for him to see me as soon as possible."

There was a small, bleak silence in the bright room. Captain Granforte looked down at his soft hands. The other three looked at Ashley standing erect and grim under the twinkling chandelier. Then Orgagna spoke:

"Captain?"

"Your Excellency?"

"You are a responsible official of high standing. I do not venture to question the wisdom or justice of your decision in this matter."

Granforte nodded acknowledgement of the careful compliment, then sat up stiffly in his chair. Orgagna went on:

"However, the case against Mr. Ashley is still far from complete and there are, as you know, certain problems, legal and—er—diplomatic, in processes against a foreign national. Mr. Ashley is a senior correspondent of world-wide reputation. He is moreover a friend of my wife and myself. I should like to make a request that, pending further investigation, Mr. Ashley be released in my custody."

Granforte's face was blank of all expression, but inside he was bubbling with satisfaction. This was the beginning of the bargain. Later there would be talk of the price. Later—much later—when there was more evidence in his hands to use as equity. He made a little play of hesitation.

"I—er—I should like to oblige Your Excellency in this matter. But there are certain problems."

"Perhaps we may be able to solve them together," said Orgagna gently.

"First is the fact that this Garofano was a citizen of the Commune. The people will expect justice to be done. It will not look well if the man who killed him remains here in the hotel, an honoured guest. It could give rise to—incidents. You understand our people— their primitive views on such things. . . ."

"I had already thought of that. I was about to suggest that Mr. Ashley come to my villa for the rest of his stay in Sorrento. I am established there, as you know, until after the election. Mr. Ashley will be private, and available for you at any time."

"Your Excellency assumes a big responsibility."

"In the name of friendship, no responsibility is too great."

Captain Granforte bowed and gave his flashing smile and turned to Ashley.

83

"Do you agree to this arrangement, Mr. Ashley?"

"I agree."

"You understand that you will be, in a moral sense, on parole?"

"I understand."

"Thank you." Granforte smiled and turned back to Orgagna. "Now, if Your Excellency could spare me a few moments, I should like to take a statement from your wife. No doubt she will feel more comfortable with you present."

"Let's do it in the other room. Help yourself to brandy, Harlequin . . . Ashley."

He turned and led the way into the bedroom, Cosima and Granforte following behind. The door closed behind them and after a moment the voices began—a low, unintelligible murmur.

Harlequin picked up the two brandy glasses, warmed them carefully over the spirit lamp on the serving-table, poured the liquor and brought it back to Ashley. They went through the wordless little ceremony, sniffing up the vapour, tasting it, feeling the slow, pervasive warmth of the liquor.

"I've underrated you, Ashley," said George Harlequin dryly.

Ashley looked at him with bleak and hostile eyes.

"Skip it, man! Skip it! I've had a bad day, remember. I'm tired."

"That's what I mean. You've been duelling with experts. You've come out of it very well."

"Whose side are you on, Harlequin?"

"Side? My dear fellow!" Harlequin's eyes were wide with innocence. "I'm on no side. My government has an interest in the outcome of the elections."

"And in Orgagna."

"That's true, too. But our views are fluid enough to . . ."

"Oh, for God's sake!" Ashley turned on his heel and walked over to the window. He stood there leaning against the steel jamb and looking out across the water to the clustered lights of the fishing-boats. The music from the lounge below drifted up to him, faint and tenuous on the still air. His body ached and his face was tight and dry. He closed his eyes and let the momentary calm steal over him and the nostalgia of the lost music. Then the flat voice spoke at his elbow:

"There's an answer, if you want it, Ashley. Assassination is out of fashion in England. We don't mind grand larceny so long as it's done according to Cocker. But we do gag on murder."

Ashley heaved himself upright and stood looking down at the little agent.

"Then you do believe that Orgagna . . ."

"I believe nothing that I can't prove," the tired voice admonished him. "I'm simply stating a principle. It might encourage you to remember it. By the way . . ."

"Yes?"

"Do you have the photostats or not?"

"Go to hell!" said Ashley wearily, and leaned back against the window-frame. They didn't change, any of them. They had no loyalty and no pity. Show them a chink in the armour and the knives were in, thrusting up towards the heart. He would trust none of them, now or ever again.

"If you haven't," said Harlequin softly, "don't let Orgagna know. They're the only weapon you've got."

Ashley said nothing. His body was heavy with weariness and his soul was sick of the warm cloying atmosphere of conspiracy. Harlequin walked away from him, his tread soundless on the thick pile of the carpet. Then the door clicked open and closed again and when Ashley looked up he was alone, a lost and puzzled man staring down at the stale bake-meats of a ducal dinner.

He opened the casement and stepped out on to the balcony. The air was very still. There was the slow, silken wash of the sea and the drift of music, louder now, with the plangent fiddles and the strumming of the soft guitars. There were the lights of Naples and the lamps of the fishermen. There were the masts of the small ships huddled under the lee of the mole. There were the villas on the cliffs and the restaurants on the capes where the visitors sat in the moonlight served by the soft-footed waiters with limpid eyes and white, flashing smiles. There was the prelude to love on the terraced walks under the orange trees. There was the commerce of love on the warm sands and in the dark grottoes under the cliffs.

They were all there, the things a man sweats out his guts to attain, to which the poor and the lazy and the irresponsible arrive ungrateful and unaware. And all of them were beyond his reach, because ambition had led him a step too far, because professional curiosity had set him digging into the muck-heap of another man's sins, because old passion had suddenly wakened and toppled him headlong into disaster.

Cosa fare? What to do about it?

Nothing, but stand here and regret and wait for other men to cast the lines of his new destiny.

Who drinks the wine of the prince must endure the prince's headache—and be thankful if the prince does not send the headsman to cure it!

There were no allies in a venture like this. There were no friends either. There were only interests, sensitive as snails to the probing fingers of the investigators. Your management didn't want truth, it wanted circulation. Your editor didn't want dossiers, he wanted headlines. Your colleagues were sceptical of crusaders and your contacts quick to see the danger of handling explosive information. So you were left alone, goaded by the perverse desire to buck the market, to prove yourself less a huckster than the rest of them, to crown your career with the halo of the apostle. You were apt to forget that apostles end up crucified, and that even Judas-pence can buy a comfortable night in

87

the tavern with the serving-girls. It takes a lifetime or a miracle to make a martyr and twenty years in the news-room makes a poor novitiate.

So you came to this—this state of isolation and suspension, where you hung like Mohammed in his little box, in a pleasureless limbo between heaven and hell.

He grinned wryly at his own discomfiture and reached for a cigarette. He lit it, smoked a few moments and found the taste of it sour and unsatisfying. He flicked it over the balcony and watched the tiny glowing tip spinning in the emptiness to be quenched finally in the grey lapping water below.

Then, suddenly, he heard the weeping.

It was low and muffled, but it was a sound so alien in this place and time that it came to him clearer than the music, clearer than the sea, the pitiful racked sobbing of a woman in grief.

He looked along the balcony. There were perhaps a dozen rooms, each opening through french windows on to the vista of sea and sky. Only four of the windows showed a light—the one he had just left, the bedroom where Cosima and Orgagna were closeted with Captain Granforte, another far down beyond them, and a fourth, just away from him at the opposite end of the balcony.

Hardly knowing why he did so—unless it were for distraction from his own ill-content—he turned towards it, moving quietly along the concrete pavement. The french window was opened slightly, but the linen curtains were drawn. He had to ease himself into position to peer into the room through a small parting between them.

He saw part of a bed with a bright, glazed counterpane, and flung across it, like a doll, the figure of a weeping girl. Her blonde hair was in disarray, her shoulders shook with sobbing and her face was buried in the rumpled pillow. But he knew her—Elena Carrese, the mannequin charmer of the afternoon, the sombre, hating beauty of the dinner-party.

He parted the curtains and stepped into the room. In two strides he had reached the bed. He sat down beside her and put his hands on her shoulders. She jerked upward and stared at him with wide, horror-stricken eyes. Her face was ugly with grief. Her voice was a terrified whisper:

"Get out! Get out of here!"

He smiled at her and patted her shoulder as one does to a child, but she thrust his hand away and recoiled from him in disgust.

"I heard you crying. I came in. If you're in trouble, I'd like to help."

"Get out, or I'll scream!"

She was so close to panic that there was no reasoning with her. Short of violence, there was no way to calm her. He got up off the bed and walked slowly towards the window. She seemed surprised by the easy victory. She watched him with fear and puzzlement. He stopped and turned back. He said, quietly:

"You promised to have coffee with me tonight. You seemed to like me then. At dinner you looked as if you hated me. Why? What are you crying about?"

She flung out her hand in a gesture of accusation. Then she began to rave at him, slack-mouthed, her face twisted, her cheeks stained and swollen with hysterical tears.

"You killed him! You and your *putana*! You killed him before he had time to ask for mercy for his poor damned soul. You killed him for a scrap of paper that . . ."

Her voice rose suddenly to wild hysteria. In one leap he was back at the bedside. He slapped her, hard, first on one cheek, then on the other. Her voice broke and she crumpled on the bed, sobbing in abject misery. Then, urgently, persistently, he began to talk to her, hoping desperately that some word or phrase would break through the barrier of animal fear and revulsion.

"Orgagna told you that, didn't he? He told you to make you hate me, to use you as a weapon against me. But he was lying. I drove the car. I was out with his wife. But I didn't kill Garofano. Orgagna killed him. He had him tossed from the embankment right under my wheels. I tried to save him. I nearly put the car over the cliff. But I was going too fast. You must believe it —for your own sake, for mine. I didn't kill him. Orgagna did that, because he wanted papers that Garofano was holding—incriminating papers. Give me time and I'll explain it. Give me time for God's sake!"

Suddenly, it seemed that he had her. Her weeping was checked. She lay a moment, face downwards, recovering herself. She dabbed at her face with the corner of the coverlet. Then, slowly, she raised herself up and looked at him.

Her eyes were full of a cold and calculating hatred. Slowly, deliberately, in the vivid obscene dialect of Naples, she began to curse him.

"May your manhood wither and your women rot. May your sons be dwarfs and your daughters barren! May you die in your sins and eat fire for all eternity, because you killed my brother!"

"Your brother!" He stared at her in amazement. His voice came out a husky whisper. "Your brother!"

Slowly, he turned away. He parted the curtains and stepped out again into the clean night air. The girl was still sitting on the bed mouthing the ritual curses of an old and secret people, calling down ruin and damnation on the man who had brought death into her family.

Blind and bedevilled, like a man in a nightmare, he walked back into the dazzling room where Cosima and Orgagna were waiting for him.

CHAPTER SIX

CAPTAIN GRANFORTE was gone, it seemed. He had taken a statement from Cosima. He had been indulgent enough to suggest that their departure for the villa might be delayed until the following morning. He was a good fellow, apt to the courtesies and not too eager to assert his authority. They were fortunate to have him handling the case. There were still many problems to be faced, but, for the present at least, an open scandal had been avoided. With discretion and co-operation, it might still be possible to . . .

The urbane voice of Vittorio d'Orgagna flowed on and on, relentlessly, while Ashley stood rocking on his feet, hearing the words as if through a blanket of cotton-wool.

". . . There are still matters of contention between us, Mr. Ashley. But your co-operative attitude this evening leads me to hope that, when we come to know each other better, we may be able to come to a suitable agreement. . . ."

"Sure, sure!"

He nodded, mechanically. Contention—co-operation—agreement! All the vague words that added up to a lie. The only words that meant anything to him now were rest and sleep.

". . . At the villa, we shall have privacy, an opportunity to talk. . . ."

Talk—talk—talk——! His head was buzzing with it. He wanted silence and darkness. He wanted time to think, time to repair his damaged strength. He said. bluntly and harshly:

"I've had enough for today—too much. I'm going to bed. Good-night, Cosima."

"Good-night, Richard." Cosima's voice was small and remote.

Orgagna took his arm and steered him solicitously to the door.

"Rest well, my dear fellow."

"Good-night, Orgagna."

He heard the door close behind him and walked slowly down the corridor and up the big marble staircase that led to his room. He fumbled wearily for his latch-key, opened the door and went in. Then he stopped dead in his tracks.

Captain Granforte was sitting in the arm-chair. He was drinking Ashley's whisky and the typescript of the Orgagna story was open on his knee.

Ashley was sick with fatigue and wordless anger. He stared at Granforte a moment, then, without a word, crossed to the table, poured himself a drink and tossed it off at a gulp. He poured another, watered it carefully, set it on the bedside-table and flung himself on the bed, pillowing his head on his hands and staring up at the ceiling.

Granforte watched him with tolerant amusement.

"Tired, my friend?"

"Yes."

"The text-books say that is the best time to question a suspect—when he is tired and his nerves are worn."

Ashley closed his eyes. The whisky lay warmly in the pit of his belly. Soon the warmth would spread, relaxing him, pervading the tired muscles, clouding the fretted brain. He wanted no argument with Granforte. He could question till he was blue in the face, he would get no more answers tonight. If he got too troublesome, he would toss him out and lock the door. The Captain spoke again. His voice was soothing and sympathetic.

"However, when one is dealing with an intelligent man, of maturity and experience, it is wiser to throw away the text-book and use tact and consideration. I know very well that I might harass you till morning and still come no nearer to the truth."

"You're a wise man, Captain," murmured Ashley. He lifted himself up on one elbow, took another drink and lay back on the pillows.

"While we were occupied downstairs, I had one of my men search your room. He found nothing to interest me, except this." He tapped the open manuscript. "I read English well enough to understand the sense of it."

94

"It's not what you're looking for, you know," said Ashley indifferently.

"No. But it does tell me something of what *you* were looking for. There are gaps preceded by notations which say: 'insert photostat 1, insert photostat 2' and so on. I should like to keep this document."

"You'll keep it whatever I say," said Ashley. "But there are two copies of it lodged with my Office in Rome."

"Who now await the final documents, before they publish it. Is that right?"

"Right. Now, please, will you get out and let me go to sleep?"

"Blackmail is a very dirty business," said Captain Granforte.

"Blackmail!" Ashley thrust himself up from the bed. "You think I'm trying to blackmail Orgagna with this story?"

"It's a strong presumption, Mr. Ashley." He held up his hand as Ashley was about to launch into a passionate denial. "Consider a moment. Why should a noble Italian, a man of wealth and influence, pretend friendship with an American journalist who is, on the evidence of this document, attempting to ruin him? Why should he offer the protection of his name and the hospitality of his house to a man who is his wife's lover?"

"You've got no right to say that!"

"Have I not, Mr. Ashley?" Granforte smiled ironically, and spread his soft hands. "On your own evidence

95

you drove this afternoon to Il Deserto, a favourite meeting place for lovers. Again, on your own evidence, you spent nearly two hours there. On the evidence of my men—taken by torchlight, I grant you—there are the tyremarks of the car leading towards the shrine. There is the grass bruised and broken over a significant area. What do you wish me to think? What contrary proposition can you offer me?"

Ashley shook his head stubbornly.

"I'm not a blackmailer. I'm not a murderer."

"You have motives for both."

"No!"

"Yes, Mr. Ashley. The murder gives you possession of documents which lead you to the possession of Orgagna's fortune and of his wife."

"You understand what you're saying? You're accusing Cosima of being an accessory to the crime?"

"I have not ignored that possibility either," said Captain Granforte coldly.

Ashley leaned forward and buried his face in his hands. The breath went out of him in a long sobbing exhalation. He was beaten and he knew it; whichever way he turned there were nets spread for him and pits dug for his unwary feet. His first impulse was to tell Granforte the whole truth and let him sort it out in his own fashion. No sooner had he thought it, than he realised it would profit him nothing. Whatever he said now could be wrenched and twisted to fit a dozen cases, all of them against himself. There was nothing to do but walk the crooked road and hope to find some light at the end of it. He raised his head and grinned wearily at Granforte.

"Do you want to take me in now, Granforte?"

The Captain looked at him oddly.

"Is that what you want, Mr. Ashley?"

"I'm too damn tired to care." It was the truest thing he had said that night, and the bitterest.

Granforte shook his head.

"When I want you, my friend, I shall know where to find you. Good-night and golden dreams!"

Granforte stood up, tossed off the last of his whisky, cocked his cap at a jaunty angle over his eyes, tucked the manuscript under his arm and walked from the room.

Richard Ashley lay on the rumpled bed, fully clothed, and stared up at the ceiling. Now at last he was alone, free from the probing malice and the buzzing voices of the inquisitors. Now he could think and try to set the jig-saw pieces into a coherent pattern.

First and most important of all, the piece around which all the rest might be keyed, was the fact that Enzo Garofano was the brother of Elena Carrese, who was the secretary and the mistress of Orgagna. The difference of names was nothing. Any man might change his name, though it might be interesting to enquire why he did it and how he managed it under the profuse documentation necessary to the simplest acts of living in Italy.

What was more important was that it established the

source of the photostats and the letters from which they came. A secretary who is also a mistress has access to a man's most private files.

But why should a woman destroy the man who kept her? Jealousy? Orgagna's history proved him a fickle lover and a ruthless one. With elections looming and the prospect of Cabinet office in a clerical state, he might find it wise to disembarrass himself of a conspicuous attachment. Perhaps this was the explanation of the presence of Tullio Ricciloli at the dinner-party. It was a feudal courtesy to arrange a marriage for the discarded girl, and in workless Italy there were suitors and to spare for a well-endowed cast-off.

It was, at face value, a feasible proposition; but it did not explain the girl's hysterical bitterness towards him and her unwillingness to accept any accusation of Orgagna—unless Orgagna had lied in this, as in so many other things. The man was subtle and experienced in the ways of women.

Perhaps at the villa he might come closer to her and turn her from an enemy into an ally.

Then he thought of Cosima, dear false lover of the old days. He remembered that she had not been questioned in his presence. She had not been confronted with his account of the accident. Her statement had been given in private, in the presence of her husband and Granforte. He wondered whether in this, too, she had betrayed him, writing him down as a liar to save herself and her husband. He thought it very likely.

Harlequin next. He of the flat voice and the pale cold eyes. He was a professional with a watching brief from his government. He was impervious to drama, unmoved by passion. The truth meant nothing to him, only the expedient. At least he had the grace to be frank about it. You knew where you stood with a man like that. Or did you?

Granforte? Granforte was a different matter altogether. Granforte was part of the system, part of Orgagna's system of privilege and preferment and . . .

His eyes closed and sleep took hold of him and he was carried off to a nightmare world where Cosima called to him from the top of a high cliff and the waves rolled over the body of a dead man, with the face of Vittorio, Duke of Orgagna.

He woke to full sunlight; but he was cramped and chilled. His evening clothes were a crumpled mess and the taste of the night's liquor and cigarettes was sour on his tongue. He heard the muted clatter of the servants and the murmur of a vacuum cleaner in the corridor outside.

He eased himself off the bed, rubbed the sleep out of his eyes, walked to the windows and threw the curtains wide. The raw sunlight dazzled him and the faint cries of the early morning bathers were a mockery of his own jaded condition. He looked at his watch—twenty past seven. There would be two or three hours to kill before the Orgagna ménage bestirred itself and made ready for the drive up to the villa.

He stripped off his clothes and walked into the bathroom to shave. The face that looked out at him from the mirror was grey and blotched with fatigue. There were dark circles under the eyes and the harsh lines of experience were etched deeper round the mouth and eyes. The chin was stubbly and the hair round the temples was flecked with the first grey streaks, an unlovely reminder that youth was passed and that maturity was less than promising.

He grimaced at himself and began to lather. When he had finished shaving, he rubbed his face with astringent, seeing with small satisfaction the colour come back into his cheeks and the slack skin tighten under the harsh liquid. A bath now and a light breakfast with copious coffee and Richard Ashley would be his own man again.

Not quite his own man—because Granforte had liens on him, and Vittorio d'Orgagna had other claims to make, and a correspondent without a story is considerably in debt to the office that underwrites his expense sheet. Still he was alive, while Enzo Garofano was dead and beyond helping. It was a small mercy and a man should be grateful for it.

As he towelled his muscular body and massaged his cropped head, he asked himself whether there were not things to be done before he left the freedom of the hotel for the hermetic atmosphere of Orgagna's villa. He wondered whether he should phone the office and tell them of the mess he was in. He decided against it. Hansen, the office chief, was a prickly, uncertain fellow, who was less concerned with the story than with the efficient administration of a news-gathering machine. He had little sympathy with eccentrics and less patience with correspondents who couldn't detach themselves from their material. Take him at the wrong moment and he was likely to haul a man off a story and order him back to Rome to answer for his indiscretions.

Besides, if he knew that the Orgagna photostats were lost, he might decide to recall the funds with the American Express, and Ashley had the idea that he might use them to some purpose. He thought he would withdraw them as soon as the office opened. It would give him something to do after breakfast.

He was half-way through dressing when the telephone rang. When he lifted the receiver and said, "*Pronto!*" Harlequin's voice answered him.

"Ashley? Sorry to call you so early."

"I was awake. I'm dressing."

"You're moving out this morning. I'd like to see you before you go—in private, that is."

"Fine. Come and have breakfast with me."

"Good. Where?"

"Come to my room. We'll take it on the balcony."

"A pleasure, my dear chap. How are you feeling?"

"Rugged."

Harlequin chuckled and hung up. Ashley set the

receiver back in its cradle and finished dressing. Then he telephoned for two breakfasts and smoked a pensive cigarette while he waited for coffee and George Harlequin.

The little man was as spry as a cricket. He chatted vapidly through the first cup of coffee and ate his breakfast as if it were the most important thing in the world. Then he sat back in his chair and looked at Ashley who was toying with a roll as if he feared it might choke him.

"I've decided to be frank with you, Ashley."

Ashley was unresponsive. He grunted:

"It's a change. Why?"

"I think there might be some profit in it."

Ashley looked up sharply. There was no irony in the pale eyes.

"Profit for whom?"

"For both of us."

Ashley scooped the remains of his roll off the table and tossed it over the balcony.

"Let's hear how frank you can be, eh?"

"Fair enough!" George Harlequin slewed his chair round and sat looking out over the sunlit water where a big white liner was steaming slowly homeward to the port of Naples. His voice was dry and impersonal. "I am as sure as you are that Garofano was murdered." He hesitated a moment and then went on. Ashley watched him narrowly. "I'm not sure who arranged it—you or Orgagna."

Ashley said nothing. For all its seeming frankness,

the statement held no news for him. Harlequin went on:

"I'm in a curious position. If you're the guilty one, I'm rather glad. It leaves me free to complete a tricky political move that advantages my government. It removes all fear of scandal and ill-timed revelations. You do see that, don't you?"

The smile he turned on Ashley was bland as a babe's.

Ashley didn't smile. This boyish fellow was colder than a fish, and he was speaking the simple truth.

"I see it, yes."

"If, on the other hand, Orgagna arranged this thing to suppress incriminating evidence against himself, then I must advise my government to wash their hands of him and withdraw from current negotiations with his colleagues. I'm in an awkward position."

"Aren't you?" said Ashley, smiling for the first time with genuine pleasure.

"We both are," said Harlequin softly. "Captain Granforte, who is a very formidable fellow, has you slated for half the crimes in the book, and he's released you as house guest to a man who hates your guts. If you're guilty, I haven't much sympathy for you. If you're innocent——" His fingers drummed a sober little rhythm on the table. "—If you're innocent, you're in a fair way to be killed like Garofano."

"Happy thought!"

"Which brings me," said Harlequin deliberately, "to

103

my question of last night. Have you the photostats or haven't you? You don't have to answer it. All I want to do is point out a simple fact. If you haven't got 'em, you're innocent, and then you need them to protect your life. Once you're out at Orgagna's place, you're tied. You need an ally to recover the photostats as quickly as possible. I'm offering my services. Always on the presumption that you didn't take 'em from Garofano when you killed him." He turned a cool and quizzical eye on Ashley, who still stared broodingly out to sea. "You still don't trust me, do you, Ashley?"

"No!"

It was as blunt as bedamned, but the little Englishman seemed to find no offence in it. He grinned disarmingly, and poured himself another cup of coffee.

"That's the trouble with the Americans. They don't understand the language."

"If you mean the diplomatic double-talk, I'll agree. We like the facts and we like them simple."

"Because you don't have to live with them, dear boy. That's our problem in Europe, we've had to live so long with so many unpleasant facts that we've developed a technique of decoration if not concealment."

"I don't see that it helps you any."

"I think it does, you know. Life can be damnably dull if you live it in four-letter words."

And for all the sourness in his mouth and the suspicion in his soul, Ashley was forced to agree with him. He laughed in spite of himself.

"So I've missed the point. Underline it for me."

"It's quite simple. Even when we talk to you in four-letter words, we still can't convince you we mean it."

Ashley hesitated a moment, then he shrugged in wry resignation.

"All right, Harlequin, I'll tell you. I haven't the photostats and I haven't a clue in the world where they are!"

George Harlequin looked at him with sober, pensive eyes.

"You've paid me a compliment. I shan't forget it. But you do worry me."

"I'm worried myself."

"Orgagna negotiated Garofano's death, and did it very neatly. He's quite capable of doing you the same service. Assassins are bought very cheaply in the back streets of Naples."

"I think he's more anxious to strike a bargain."

"Only because he believes you have the photostats."

Ashley leaned forward across the table.

"You said that before. That's why I mistrusted you. He must know that I haven't got them."

George Harlequin looked puzzled.

"I don't see that."

"It's quite simple. Cosima was with me every minute from the time I quarrelled with Garofano in the lounge till the time I picked him off the road and brought him back to Sorrento. Do you mean to tell me she hasn't accounted to Orgagna for every second and every minute of those hours, with the possible exception of the love passages?"

George Harlequin looked at him in blank amazement.

"Do you believe that?"

"Any reason why I shouldn't?"

"You poor, unhappy fool," said Harlequin softly. "Don't you know she's in love with you?"

Ashley shook his head and stared sombrely at the backs of his brown strong hands.

"She sold me out, Harlequin. She sold me out twice to the same man. I could never trust her again."

Harlequin shrugged fastidiously.

"It's your own business, of course. And I don't know the lady very well. A pity. You need a friend in the Orgagna household."

"I hope to have one," said Ashley briskly, and he began to tell him of Elena Carrese and how she had cursed him as the murderer of her brother.

Harlequin gave a low whistle of surprise, then settled down to listen intently. When Ashley had finished, he got up, walked to the railing and stood a long time looking out over the shining water. Then he sat down again, leaned across the table and began a low, earnest exposition.

"I warned you at the beginning that you were dealing with matters you did not understand. I think you understand them better now, but you are still on alien ground. You are in an old and complex country where nothing is as simple as it looks on the surface. You must learn to think in paradoxes. Elena Carrese, for instance. You meet her as a sophisticate from Rome, and yet she curses you like a peasant in the runic language of the South. To her family—if she has any—she is a *putana*, because she has renounced her virtue to share the bed of a duke. Yet she weeps for a seedy little pedlar because he was her brother. You consider her motives, and you choose the one that suits your own habit of mind: jealousy. I could name you twenty others, each of them twice as strong. These are an old people, Ashley, the end product of two thousand years of misrule and civil disorder and recurrent conquest. They are bound by beliefs to which you are a stranger. They bow to traditions which to you are laughable but to them are more binding than the Decalogue. Unless you realise that, you will fall into errors that may well destroy you."

"Does that apply to Orgagna, too?"

"Most of all," said George Harlequin gravely, "it applies to Orgagna. I have seen what you have written about him, and all of it is true. He is a financial manipulator, an unscrupulous politician, an adventurer with ambition to rule. But that is not the whole truth, because you cannot write two thousand years of history in a single sentence. A man like Orgagna is not explained with adjectives. He is not damned by a dozen documents like yours. I cannot explain him to you.

Your only hope is to have him explain himself. And then . . ."

He broke off as if at a loss for words.

Ashley prompted him, quietly.

"He begins to explain himself. What then?"

"Then, my dear fellow, you will understand why I fear for you."

CHAPTER SEVEN

WHEN HARLEQUIN HAD LEFT HIM, Ashley packed his bags and left them strapped and ready for the porters. He went downstairs and paid his bill and walked briskly round to American Express to withdraw the two thousand dollars. He presented his passport and signed the quittance and the clerk handed over twenty hundred-dollar notes, crisp and new from the presses. Ashley counted them and shoved them into his wallet.

Then the clerk handed him a letter. It was postmarked at Rome and bore the office symbol. When he opened it, he found two minute clippings from the continental edition of the *New York Times*. The first was a two-line teaser from a gossip columnist:

What press baron is slated for what diplomatic appointment and why?

The second was a brief paragraph with a London date-line:

Mr. Charles Langdon, London Office Chief of the Monitor chain, has been awarded the O.B.E. for conspicuous service in the furthering of international understanding through the medium of the press and news services.

The clippings were pinned to a sheet of office note-paper, on which was scrawled in Hansen's dashing, violent script: "Up the Press! There's hope for us yet!"

Ashley grinned at the little professional gag. He was in the wrong company it seemed. Birthday honours and diplomatic appointments were reserved for sober citizens who drove carefully and kept their hands free of the smuts of scandal. He shoved the envelope into his pocket and walked out into the clear dry sunshine of the square.

The morning traffic was milling round the big bronze statue of Saint Antonino, patron of the town, who looked down with a tolerant smile on the motley crowd of visitors who fed his people during the summer and helped them to live a step or two further from starvation during the harsh winter. They came in all shapes, sizes and nationalities—the brown girls in bright sun-frocks with bare shoulders and proud young heads crowned with crazy straw hats, the long-legged boys in denim shorts and flowered shirts, sober Germans in cream suits and heavy clod-hopping shoes, dowdy women from the French provinces and sleek young cavaliers from Rome on the look-out for an American wife.

They were hurrying down to the Marina to catch the morning boat to Capri. They were writing postcards at the little table on the pavement. They were turning over the lace-work and the inlaid boxes on the trays outside the tourist shops. They were sitting near the little rotunda under the orange trees, drinking coffee and eating sweet biscuits. They were bargaining with the taxi-men and the *cocchieri* for a cut-price drive to Positano or a leisurely clip-clop run down to Massa Lubrense.

Waiters in espadrilles and striped cotton coats were washing down the marble-tops of the tables in the bars. Peasant women padded along in wooden sandals, with big glass jars or bundles of washing on their heads. The couriers were standing at the bus stop, resplendent in braided caps, and a policeman in a green uniform with a black gun on his hip blew his whistle and waved his arms helplessly at the traffic piled up round the feet of Saint Antonino.

It was gay, inconsequent and charming, and Richard Ashley felt as remote from it as the man in the moon.

He stood to one side of the big iron gates that opened into the hotel gardens and smoked a leisurely cigarette. A shabby fellow sidled up to him and offered American cigarettes at a hundred lire under the market. Ashley waved him away. The chances were they were made in a back-yard factory in Naples from the butts which the beggars picked out of the stinking gutters.

An old woman thrust a knotted filthy hand under his nose, beseeching alms. He dug into his pocket for a handful of coins and she moved away, blessing him wheezily in the name of God and the blessed Virgin and the twenty-eight saints of Sorrento.

An optimistic pedlar tried to sell him a straw hat. A little schoolgirl offered him a posy to buy for the local convent. A restaurant tout waved a brochure under his nose and wanted to change his money. Then he saw Roberto, the barman.

He was crossing the square from the direction of the petrol station. His head was down and he was hurrying like a man who is late for work. Ashley watched him come and as he entered the big iron gates, fell into step beside him.

"Good-day, Roberto!"

Roberto looked up, startled, and gave him a nervous smile and a mumbled good-morning. He tried to quicken his pace, but Ashley caught at his wrist and drew him off the path among the palm trees. It was a shady spot, half-screened from the path, with a tiny pergola where middle-aged tourists came to sit and drink *aranciata* when the afternoon sun drove them under shelter.

Roberto tried to pull himself away, but Ashley held him and twisted his wrist, forcing him under the pergola and out of view by passers-by. Roberto looked up at him with frightened eyes.

"*Signore*, I beg of you . . . for the love of God! I am late for work. Please, what do you want with me?"

Ashley wrenched his arm up into hammerlock and with his free hand hauled him back against his chest and held him, with his wrist hard against his throat and his fist forcing his head backward. Roberto gasped and tried to struggle, but the pain was too much for him and he relaxed, sweating and trembling against Ashley's chest.

"If you do that again," said Ashley softly, "I'll dislocate your arm, understand?"

"*Capito!*" It was a whisper of abject terror.

"You gave me a message yesterday, Roberto. It was a message of warning. I was to take what was offered but to trust the offerer not at all. I paid you five thousand lire for that. Now I want to know more. Who gave you the message?"

Roberto was trembling with fear. Ashley could feel his heart pounding under the skinny rib-case.

"Who gave you the message?"

"I—I don't know the man, *signore.*"

"You're lying." He jerked the imprisoned arm and Roberto gasped and choked as the wrist closed on his wind-pipe. Ashley was ashamed of his brutality but his own life was at stake. He had no time to be squeamish. "Who was the man? What was his name?"

"There—there was no name, *signore.* It was a man I have not seen before. From Naples, possibly. He gave me the message and an envelope with ten thousand lire."

"What else?"

"He—he also gave me the telephone number."

"What number?" In his excitement, he tightened his grip and Roberto gave a high, animal squeal.

"Please, *signore*, please! You will kill me. I am trying to tell you."

"The telephone number!"

"This—this was the number I was to ring, if you left the hotel. I was to say what time you left and with whom. I was to say also where, if I knew."

"And you did that?"

"Yes, *signore*."

"When?"

"After you went out with Her Excellency."

"What was the number?"

"I—I have forgotten it, *signore*."

"Remember!"

"It was . . . Sorrento 673."

"Anything else?"

"No, *signore*! Nothing! There was nothing more. I swear it on the bones of my mother and the grave of my father."

"Why should he give you a message that means nothing?"

"I—I do not know, *signore*."

"Guess!"

"To—to make trouble between you—mistrust."

"To provoke a quarrel?"

"It was suggested."

"Which you would report in the same way to the same number?"

"Yes, *signore*."

"If you're lying, Roberto . . ."

"*Signore*—for pity! I swear that you have had the truth."

He released him then and watched him scuttle away, rubbing his bruised throat, massaging the wrenched muscles of his shoulder. He didn't blame him too much. It was part of the trade in this country—the small profit for petty intrigue. Times were hard in Italy and a man could give small thought to the morals of an act that put ten thousand lire in his pocket and fed a wife and three *bambini*.

Ashley smoothed down his rumpled jacket, straightened his tie and walked thoughtfully back to the square. He crossed in front of the statue of the benign Saint Antonino and made his way to a small bar just beyond the petrol station. He walked in, bought a slug from the attendant, and went to the telephone in the corner.

Carefully, he dialled the numerals 6—7—3. He heard the jangling characteristic note of Italian receivers. Then the ringing stopped and a man's voice said:

"*Pronto!*" Villa Orgagna!"

Ashley hung up the receiver and walked out of the bar. The heat was beginning to beat up from the pavements and from the stuccoed walls of the houses. He shivered like a man who had just looked into his own grave.

When he reached the hotel he found the blue Isotta drawn up in front of the entrance and, behind it, a small estate car into which the aproned porters were stacking luggage, watched by a chauffeur in dark-blue uniform.

The manager was going through an elaborate ceremony of farewell with Cosima and Orgagna, while Elena Carrese and Tullio Riccioli stood a little apart, talking in low tones.

They looked up when he entered and greeted him with the constrained smiles that politeness demanded. His arrival shortened the leave-taking and, two minutes later, they were piling into the Isotta—Orgagna and Cosima in front, Tullio and Ashley in the back, with the girl between them.

Orgagna swung the big car out of the drive, eased it through the alleys and across the square and soon they were heading up the rise and over the shoulder, along the high winding road that led westward to the end of the peninsula.

The hood was down and the wind of their swift progress ruffled their hair and blew gratefully in their faces, but the grey olives hung motionless in the heat and the shrill chorus of the cicadas sounded above the deep purring of the engine and the whip of the tyres over the metalled road. The sky was a dazzle in the eyes and the sea was a blue miracle beyond the grey thrust of the cliffs and the nestling of the fisher villages in the small crescent beaches.

On their left, the hills climbed steeply to the spine of the mountains and the olives and orange trees marched over them like grey-green armies. On the right, the land was terraced to the cliff-edge and, where the trees were sparse, there were the garden-plots of the peasant farmers, cabbage and onions and the tall knobbed stalks of the artichokes.

Thick-bodied peasant women bent among them, and bare-legged boys and tattered girls waved and shouted as the big car swept past them. Donkey carts trundled along the verge of the road, and they passed an occasional *carozza* with its plumed horse and its load of conscientious sight-seers.

Orgagna was in a good humour. He drove fast and expertly. His face in the rear-vision mirror was smiling as he pointed out the landmarks and made little jokes about the local oddities. He was at pains to make himself agreeable and the others responded with more and more freedom—all except Elena Carrese who sat, stiff and unresponsive, between Tullio and Ashley.

At last they came to a small, cobbled turning. Orgagna swung the car into it and they drove down a winding lane hung with olive trees to a pair of great iron gates flanked by high tufa walls. When the car stopped, Ashley could see the big metal bosses, with the sculptured crest of the House of Orgagna.

Orgagna sounded his horn and an old, gnarled fellow with tousled hair and a wizened face came trotting to open the gates. He swung them back and dropped the bolts, then came to Orgagna. His old lips framed a blessing and he seized his master's hand and kissed it. Orgagna smiled at him and returned his blessing in dialect and rumpled his hair with an affectionate gesture.

Then he eased the car up the long, gravelled drive to the villa.

The first sight of the place was a shock to Ashley. By some trick of association he had imagined it as one of those white, square boxes with blind walls and Moorish arches, canted out on the hillsides of Capri. He had thought of it as a holiday resort with bright shutters and striped awnings and candy-stick umbrellas spread over cane tables on the terrace.

Instead it reared itself up—three storeys of baroque magnificence, with curlicued balconies and great carved doors, with a wide terrace and a marble balustrade below which the rockeries dropped away to green lawns, which spread themselves out to the fringe of the orange gardens and the olive-groves.

Ancient pines towered over the roof-top, and below them was the feathery drooping of palms and the brighter green of shade trees. The flower-beds were ablaze with colour and beyond them was the rich blue of the Mediterranean.

As Orgagna brought the car to a stop, the big panelled doors swung open and a tall grey-haired fellow in the livery of a major-domo came forward to meet them. Behind him Ashley could see half a dozen servants, male and female, lining the wide hall. It was a princely homecoming for His Excellency the Duke of Orgagna.

The major-domo helped them out of the car, Orgagna first, then Cosima, then the others, giving to each a carefully judged portion of respect and welcome.

When he came to Elena Carrese, he took her in his arms, kissed her on both cheeks and held her a moment against his braided chest. The girl clung to him in childish pleasure and Ashley thought she was going to burst into tears.

Orgagna caught his look of surprise and smiled.

"The steward of my house—Carlo Carrese. Elena is his daughter."

"Oh!"

It wasn't a very intelligent comment, but what else was there to say? He was hedged about with mysteries and Orgagna's domestic relationships were the biggest mystery of all.

Finally the flurry of the greetings was over and Ashley was led upstairs to a big square room with a four-poster bed and a coffered ceiling, whose windows looked over the olive trees to a small, circular bay with a shoulder of cliff behind.

The shutters were open; the room was full of sun and, when the servant had gone, Ashley stood in the middle of the tiled floor and took stock of his surroundings.

The room was big enough to deploy an army. Even the great bed was dwarfed by it. The ceiling was rich with gold leaf and the tiles of the floor were patterned with rose petals, so delicately done that he was tempted to reach down and touch them. The chests and wardrobes were made by Florentine craftsmen and the overmantel was a baroque masterpiece in mottled marble. The opulence of it would have oppressed him had it not been for the sunlight streaming in through the big french windows.

He was reminded once again that he was an alien—a man from the new world, strange and uneasy among the surviving splendours of the old

There was a knock at the door and another maid-servant came in, lumping his suitcase and his overnight bag. He made a move to help her, but she refused, smiling, and began to unpack, laying out suits and linen, setting aside his soiled clothes for laundering.

He stood, smoking a cigarette and watching her, finding a surprising pleasure in the sight of her thick body and her broad simple face and her work-stained hands busy over the humble, human service. In the wild unreality of his situation, she was his first link with reality and he was grateful to her. He asked her:

"*Come ti chiam'?* What's your name?"

"Concetta."

"Have you worked here long?"

Her head went up in a little gesture of pride and she smiled, broadly.

"*Son' della famiglia, signore.* I belong to the family. I am the servant of the Duchessa. She has asked me to look after you."

"The Duchessa is very kind."

"*C'e una cara*—a dear one, *signore.*"

She picked up the soiled linen, stuffed it into the overnight bag and left the room.

C'e una cara—a dear one indeed! Dear and desirable

—and damned expensive to a man who has come to the middle years and finds that he has no more love to spend, but must husband it carefully like the oil in a flickering lamp. The cynics might make a dirty joke of a thought like that. Yet it was true. The years might tame the body, but they left the soul still hungry. And the love dried out of it as the sap dried out of a tree and left it dying from the top. A man might die alone, by accident or act of God. But if he died unloved, then he died poor indeed.

It was a morbid thought and he tried to thrust it away. He slipped off his jacket, undid his tie and knotted a coloured scarf round his neck. Then he walked downstairs and out on to the sunlit terrace.

Orgagna was there, cool and scrupulously groomed in holiday clothes. He was leaning on the marble balustrade, staring seaward across the green fall of the land. At the sound of Ashley's footfall he looked up and smiled a greeting.

"Come and join me, Ashley. You're comfortably settled?"

"Very comfortably, thank you."

"You like my place?"

"I like it very much. I envy you."

"Walk with me a while and let me show it to you."

"Surely."

There was so much friendliness in his smile, such genuine pleasure in his voice, that it was hard to believe he was the man who had plotted a murder to conceal a succession of criminal acts. In an odd fashion, Ashley found himself grateful to him. To live here in open hostility would have been an intolerable strain.

Orgagna took his arm and led him along the terrace to a flight of stone steps flanked by twin marbles—a dancing faun and a bacchante in the smooth, bloodless style of Canova. The steps led them on to a gravelled path which wound through the lawns and into the orange groves, downward towards the sea.

As they walked, Orgagna talked to him, no longer in the smooth devious phrases of the diplomat, but simply, quietly, as a man wanting to share the pleasures of his homecoming.

"Whenever I come back to this place—which now, is all too seldom—I feel that I am a boy again. I was born here, you see. I played under these same olive trees. I learned to swim from the beach down there. I caught my first fish from the rocks under the cape—a big *scorfano*, bright red. He weighed nearly a kilo. I have a place in Rome. I have houses in other parts of Italy. But to me, this is home. Can you understand that?"

"Sure. There's only one place that's home, to any of us."

"Long before the House of Savoy, long before the Bourbons and the Kingdom of the Two Sicilies, before Amalfi was the first republic of Italy, my family owned this land on which you walk. Up on the cliffs you will see the ruins of the old towers which my ancestors built in the time of the Barbary raiders. It is a long history and a turbulent one. We have lost, we have gained. But all through it, we have held this land. Our peasants have farmed it. Our fisherfolk have plied its waters. We have built our houses and have seen them destroyed, by time, war and earthquakes; but always we have rebuilt. The servants have been the sons of the servants of our fathers. Our lawns are green over the bodies of many dead. Our flowers blossom out of the compost of history. It . . . it is something to remember, *non è vero?*"

"Much," said Ashley soberly. "Almost too much."

Orgagna looked at him oddly and gave him a small, enigmatic smile.

"It pleases me to hear you say that, Ashley. It shows an understanding heart, even though you do not always wear it on your sleeve. I will admit it to you. Sometimes it is almost too much. Do you know why?"

Orgagna did not give him the answer immediately, but led him down a small alleyway, between low-hanging trees. At the end of the alley was a low wall, below which the ground dropped steeply away to a small plateau of black fertile soil where a couple of peasant families were tilling the vegetable rows. A clutter of grimy children looked up and shouted a greeting. Orgagna laughed at them and waved back. Then his face clouded and he turned to Ashley.

"There is the reason, Ashley. The children. Cosima has never given me a child. I am the last of the line.

With me the name of Orgagna dies—and all the past dies too."

"There's time yet," said Ashley, carefully.

"When there is not enough love," said Orgagna softly, "there is never enough time."

He leaned his elbows on the stone coping of the wall and stared out across the valley.

"It is the thing that drives us all, this desire to establish a permanent foothold on the earth from which death must ultimately dislodge us. It is the thing that drives us from one woman to another, from one ambition to another. We are the sad bulls, Ashley, blind with the desire to perpetuate ourselves, before our strength deserts us and the young ones close in to gore us to death."

The cicadas shrilled their wild, persistent song. Lizards sunned themselves on the stones. Far down among the olive trees a bird sang, high and clear, and another answered him faintly from the hill. The two men stood looking out across the valley where the heat rose trembling in the summer air. Then Orgagna straightened up and smiled apologetically.

"I embarrass you, my friend. Forgive me. Let us finish our walk."

Linking his arm in Ashley's, continental fashion, he led him out of the alley and on to the long winding path that led to the cliffs and to the ruined tower that his ancestors had built against the Saracens.

It took Ashley a little time to understand what Orgagna was driving at. His Excellency was preparing his defence. So far, at least, it was an impressive piece of work.

Impressive, too, was the efficiency with which the Orgagna acres were being farmed. Ashley was all too familiar with the depressed standards of agricultural communities in southern Italy—the primitive, wasteful methods, the impoverishment of blood-stock, the wearing out of the land with over-cropping and under-nourishment. He had seen it among the small-holders. He had seen it on the big estates in Puglia and Calabria, whose landlords let their stewards bleed the land to pay for their villas at Frascati and their big cabin-cruisers at Rapallo.

Here, it was not so. Old trees were being grubbed out and the land carefully fallowed. The wood was sawn and stacked into piles to dry. There were rows of young trees, carefully planted and scientifically sprayed. The irrigation channels were free of weeds and the orange trees were new strains imported from Australia and California.

When Ashley commented on it, Orgagna gave him a sidelong smile.

"It surprises you, Ashley? Why should it?"

"It's rare in this part of the world."

"All too rare, I agree," said Orgagna gravely. "But you cannot change a whole country overnight. You cannot, in five years—ten, twenty years—eradicate the ignorance and superstition of centuries. You need education for that. You need educators. You need communications, roads, bridges, power lines, telephones, to carry the education to depressed areas."

Ashley nodded. So much was evident. It was not so evident what Orgagna was going to make of the argument. For the moment it seemed he was prepared to drop it. He walked Ashley through the last fringes of trees to a stretch of rough grass-land that ran right down to the edge of the cliff. The ground was rough and stony and the grass grew brown and wiry through the sparse top-soil. A small herd of goats cropped lazily through it, watched by an old gnarled shepherd seated on a rock forty paces away.

Orgagna pointed him out to Ashley.

"Look well at him, my friend. Understand him and you will begin to understand our problem in this country. He is sixty years old, though he looks eighty. He has been doing this since he was ten. He cannot read or write. If you talked to him in Italian, he would not understand a word you said—and his tongue would be a mystery to you also. He has lived here all his life, not ten miles from Sorrento, yet I doubt whether he has been there more than a dozen times. Ask him why and he will tell you that life here has been good to him and he sees no reason to change it. He has been happy in his own fashion; he sees no reason why the same happiness should not suffice for his children and his children's children. He, and hundreds of thousands like him, are the biggest problem we have in Italy today."

"I don't agree," said Ashley flatly.

Orgagna looked up sharply.

"Why not?"

For a long moment Ashley was silent. The words had come, unweighed and unconsidered. But now that they were spoken, he knew that they had brought him to the moment of decision. Should he go on playing this undignified game of hints and allusions? Should he go on living in the house of an enemy, eating his salt, remembering that he had been in love with his wife, smiling at him across the wine and hating him and planning to destroy him? Or should he end it here and now, cards on the table, betting strength against strength.

Orgagna repeated his question.

"Why not?"

"Because this man," he gestured towards the old shepherd, "and others like him are to be found all over the world—in English villages, in the Catskill mountains, riding the boundaries in Australia, plodding round the polders in Holland. The responsibility for the future doesn't rest with them. It rests with men who have at their disposal education, influence, wealth and power, and who, too often, use them for their own profit and not for the benefit of their people."

It was out now and he was glad of it. Dignity was restored to him. The next move was up to Orgagna.

But Orgagna was not to be drawn. He was too subtle for that, too wise to make an ill-timed quarrel with a man who still held power over him. He turned away from the old shepherd and pointed to the crumbling square pile of the watch-tower perched on the hump of the cliff. His voice was quiet and controlled.

"Look at the tower, Ashley. The man who built that was my lineal ancestor. His name was the same as mine —Vittorio. He was an unpleasant fellow, as I probably am myself. He was a ruffian, a tippler, a lecher. He fathered a whole brood of bastards on the girls of the village. Yet his people loved him. His name is a legend still. Do you know why? Because when the raiders came with their long galleys and the fires blazed in the watch-towers, he gathered his mercenaries together and armed his peasants with axes and bill-hooks and drove them back, fighting himself in the front of the battle. What matter that he drank? What matter that he taxed them to the bone and flogged the payments out of them and seduced a girl or two? He had kept the land safe, had he not? And they knew that in the end it is only the land that matters. He was the strong one and they needed his strength—as they need it now, Ashley! As they will always need it!"

And with that Orgagna turned on his heel and left him, walking swiftly up towards the trees, scattering the bleating goats, trampling the brown and tired grass.

Ashley looked at the old stone tower, broken and crumbling but still foursquare to the winds and to the sea. He saw the whole intricate fabric of the big story waver and tilt like a house of cards.

CHAPTER EIGHT

THE SUN was searing his eyeballs. The heat rose from the ground and parched his face. Runnels of sweat formed on his body and stained the thin fabric of his shirt. His scarf began to prickle and stifle him. He decided he could use a swim. He walked to the edge of the cliff and looked down.

A narrow, stony path led down the sloping face to a beach of black sand, broken at intervals by rocky outcrops. The water was clear and clean and from where he stood he could see the waving of sea-grasses and the bloom of rock-flowers in pools of sapphire and emerald. The rocks jutted out into the water and there were ledges where a man might sun himself and deep hollows where he might dive in safety.

He stepped back from the cliff-edge and began to scramble down the path. The pebbles rolled and rattled dryly down the incline. He put his hand against the rock wall to steady himself and cursed as the hot stone scorched his palms. Then he trod on a loose stone, his feet slid from under him and he slid the last dozen yards on the seat of his trousers, to land, gasping and cursing, on the beach.

Then he heard Cosima laughing.

She was stretched on a big beach-towel under the lee of the rocks, her brown body sun-drenched and beautiful. Her eyes were hidden by dark glare-glasses, but her lips were laughing and her shoulders shook with merriment at his comic arrival.

He picked himself up, dusted off the sand and sat down beside her.

Suddenly, the laughter was quenched. She heaved herself up and clung to him desperately, head against his breast, sobbing with passionate relief.

"Oh, Richard! *Caro mio!* I thought you might come. I hoped it. But there was no time to ask you. This is the first time I've been left alone since yesterday. There's so much to say . . . so many things to explain. . . . Kiss me, *caro mio*!"

And, because he was committed to the crooked road, because he could not waste even the false information she would give him, because he needed time to think, and because, in spite of himself, she still stirred him, he kissed her. Her skin was silken under his hands. Her lips were soft against his mouth. Her whole body surrendered to him. Then, slowly, she released him and lay back again on the towel, head pillowed on her arms, looking up at him.

He said, lamely enough, "I've been out walking with your husband. He left me and went back to the house. I thought I'd like a swim."

"A lucky thought, Richard. We can swim together."

"We'd better talk first."

He peeled off his shirt and tossed it on the sand. Cosima sat up and clasped her arms round her knees. She was looking at him, but he could not see her eyes. He reached out and took off the sun-glasses. She blinked in the sudden glare, but made no move to put them on again. Her eyes were grave and tender. To him they were full of lies.

"We must talk, mustn't we?"

"Yes."

"It was horrible yesterday, Richard—the questions, the long duelling discussions, the lies, the comedy I had to play to show I didn't love you any more, that I didn't care what happened to you."

He smiled at her and said, gently:

"You played it very well."

There were lies in his own eyes, too. Lies to which she had committed him and for which he could forgive neither her nor himself. He scooped up a little handful of sand and let it trickle through his fingers on to her skin. He questioned her, gently:

"What does your husband think—about us?"

"Nothing, Richard. That we are, or have been lovers, is of little importance to him. Between him and me there has been no love for a long time. Where my heart leans, he does not care. But as his wife, I am important to him—politically. You are important because you have it in your power to ruin him."

"Why the comedy then?"

131

"For Captain Granforte, for George Harlequin . . . even, I think, for Tullio and Elena."

"Why for them? Elena's his mistress, isn't she?"

Cosima smiled ruefully.

"She was. Now, she has become inconvenient to him. She will be out of place in Cabinet circles. Before we left Rome, he told her there was hope of reconciliation between us. My meeting with you destroyed the fiction, but my husband insists it be kept up. That's why he brought Tullio down. He wants him to marry her."

Ashley grinned sardonically:

"Tullio's tastes don't run to women."

"Therefore it is unimportant whether he marries or not. The important thing is that he will be paid for it."

"Won't Elena have something to say about that?"

Cosima made a little gesture of distaste and weariness.

"Less than you think, Richard. There are many girls like her in this country, and too few men who can afford to marry them. She has two courses open to her —find another protector, or marry Tullio and enjoy the money my husband will settle on her, and the freedom of a neglected wife. I think she will prefer the latter."

"Is she in love with your husband?"

"That's the pity of it, Richard," said Cosima soberly. "I believe she is. I am very, very sorry for her."

Ashley was beginning to be pleased with himself. There was profitable information here; and so far there

132

were no lies. He thought it would not be long before the lying began. At least he would have the satisfaction of knowing it. He framed the next questions with elaborate care.

"Cosima, you know the position I'm in, don't you?"

"Only too well, Richard. That's why I'm afraid for you."

"You understand that every answer you give me is important, even though it seems trivial and irrelevant."

"Yes."

"Fine. Now tell me, what was I trying to buy from Garofano?"

"Photostats of certain letters written by my husband."

"How do you know that?"

"You told me you were buying information. My husband told me what it was."

"When?"

"After I came back from—from the accident."

"How did he know?"

"I don't know that. All I know is that ever since this investigation started he has been kept informed of your movements and your contacts. That . . . that wouldn't be hard, would it?"

"Do you know who Garofano was?"

"No. I heard the Captain say that he was a clerk from Naples. That's all."

"Does your husband know?"

"If he does, he didn't say."

"Why did you want me to lie about the accident?"

Her eyes widened with doubt and surprise at the unexpected question, but she answered it without hesitation.

"I told you that, Richard. It is unwise to make drama with the police here. And I was right, wasn't I?"

"Yes, you were right. Now tell me, why did your husband bring me here when he might have left me in the hands of the police?"

Cosima looked at him sombrely.

"Because I think—I fear—that he may be himself involved in the death of this man."

The bluntness of it surprised him. But he said nothing. Cosima went on:

"Even if he were not involved, he would wish to avoid a scandal involving me, and, therefore, involving himself. It would be untimely and dangerous to his career. More than this——" She stumbled a moment. "—More than this, he believes you have the photostats. He wants to bargain with you, or force you to return them to him."

It seemed to him so patent and unnecessary a lie that he forgot to be cautious. He thrust away from her and snapped:

"Goddammit, Cosima, you don't believe that. Neither do I. He must know I haven't got them. You saw Garofano refuse to sell them to me. You were with me every moment from then till the time I brought you back to the hotel. You must have told your husband what happened."

Quietly and firmly she gave him the answer.

"I told him, yes. I told him that I had seen you struggle with Garofano and take an envelope from his breast pocket. He believed me, Richard."

"Why did you tell him that?"

"If not, you would now be in jail—or waiting for a death like Garofano."

He looked up and saw the wonderment and pain in her face. He knew then what a fool he had been—and promptly made himself a bigger one. He drew her to him and held her close and tried to apologise for his folly.

"Cosima, I—I can't say how sorry I am. I should have known you wouldn't lie to me. I was afraid you'd sold me out and——"

She wrenched herself out of his arms and struck him, once and again, across the mouth. She snatched up her wrap and towel and stood looking down at him, her breast heaving with anger, her eyes blazing with contempt.

"You—you could believe that! You could believe it and still hold me in your arms and kiss me and ... You are foul and filthy! Filthy like the rest of them! I wish to God I had never known you!"

She scooped up a handful of sand and flung it full in his eyes and went racing up the shingly path towards the comforting shadow of the olive trees.

Blind and despairing, Richard Ashley stumbled down to the water's edge and tried to wash the sand out of his eyes.

"Women!" said Tullio Riccioli, in his drawling precious voice. "Women are an infernal nuisance. Love them and they cheat you—or send you bankrupt with a brood of squalling *bambini*. Ignore them and they throw themselves into your arms. A man should live on a desert island with a paint-box and a sympathetic friend."

"Tullio, I think you've got something!" said Ashley.

Tullio had been painting on the terrace and Ashley had stumbled into him as he came back to the house, his eyes scalding and scarred. Tullio had made no fuss, but whisked him upstairs and out of range of embarrassing enquiries. Now he was in his room, sitting in a low chair, head canted back, while Tullio's soft, womanish hands probed for the sharp sand crystals and bathed his smarting eyeballs with olive oil. It was difficult to talk with his head thrown back and his throat muscles stretched, but any talk was a relief from the torment of loneliness and self-accusation.

"You quarrelled with her, did you?"

"I apologised to her."

"A singular folly," said Tullio calmly. "You are old enough to know better."

He sponged the upturned lids with cotton-wool and dropped warm oil over the inflamed conjunctiva.

Ashley sighed with relief as the lids settled back without the searing pain.

"Thanks, Tullio. I'm very grateful."

Tullio wiped his hands on a silk handkerchief.

"A pleasure, my friend. We all need allies against the ladies. It sickens me to think what a man must go through for the privilege of having children who will later kick him in the teeth."

"They tell me you're going through it yourself very soon."

"Oh that!" Riccioli shrugged fastidiously, and wrinkled his fine patrician nose. "That is a matter of business—tedious but necessary. Once it is over . . ." He waved a delicate hand in dismissal. "*Finito!* That's the end of it."

"The island, the paint-box and the sympathetic friend?"

"Precisely. Does it shock you?"

"Nothing shocks me any more," said Ashley, with considerable conviction. "But I'd be interested to know how you made the bargain. It sounds like a profitable business."

Tullio fished in his breast pocket, brought out a miniature manicure set and addressed himself to the delicate business of buffing his finger-nails.

"It started with Carla Manfredi. Perhaps you know her? She's a bitch but loaded with money. She sponsored my first exhibition. We got very good notices, even if we didn't sell very much. I wanted her to do

137

another but by that time she'd lost interest in art and turned to music. He's a Pole, I believe. Carla thinks he's a second Paderewski. However, she did suggest that I try Orgagna. She arranged for us to meet at a party, and later I talked to him at his office. He's quite happy to finance me—on these terms. They're quite generous really. Though I do suspect Elena's getting a lot more out of it than I am. Wouldn't you say that?"

"I think it's very probable," said Ashley, with ready sympathy. "As you say, women are a nuisance, but they seem to get the best of most bargains."

Riccioli looked up sharply in fear of being laughed at, but Ashley's face was blankly serious. He smiled at Ashley.

"You're not making much profit yourself, are you?"

Ashley made a rueful little mouth and looked shrewd.

"A little—but not enough. I'm prepared to lay out money to make more."

"How much?"

The limpid, girlish eyes were hard and calculating. Tullio Riccioli might be the spoiled darling of the *salons* and the fastidious friend of the æsthetes, but he'd started life in a Roman slum and he was certain he was never going back.

"A thousand dollars," said Ashley coolly. "Up or down according to the service."

"Name it, *signore*!" Tullio made him an elaborate pantomime of service.

"Later, Tullio, later!" Ashley's smile was bland as

butter. "I thought you'd be interested to know the money was up."

"Money's the only thing that does interest me. Money and painting."

"What about the sympathetic friend?"

"That's what the money's for," said Tullio innocently.

Then the gong sounded for lunch and they walked out of the room together, chuckling like a pair of conspirators. In spite of his damaged eyes and Cosima's damaged pride, Ashley thought he would enjoy his meal.

He had useful information and the promise of more in the near future. More than that, he had an ally, bound to him by the strongest chain of all—money.

Lunch was a desultory meal served under the big vine pergola in an angle of the terrace. They ate reclined on the canvas chairs, while the servant girls hurried from one to another with plates of food, and Carlo Carrese stood, like an attendant Gorgon, by the ice-bucket where the heady white wine of the Orgagna vintage lay cooling in round-bellied bottles.

They were languid with sun and content to drowse over the meal. They were uneasy with each other, so that conversation flagged quickly and Ashley, remote behind a pair of sun-glasses, was able to study their faces and their attitudes.

The old major-domo interested him most of all. His attitude was one of deferential service to each, but for

Orgagna he reserved a special, almost paternal solicitude, settling the cushions at his back, questioning him on the quality of the wine and the dishes, watching for the slightest gesture of request.

He must have been nearly seventy, Ashley thought; but his back was straight, his hands were steady and he moved as lightly and as swiftly as a young man. His face was lined and weathered like a rock. There were deep furrows about his eyes and his mouth was tight and firm. His great hooked nose and his black, flashing eyes gave him a curious resemblance to Orgagna himself.

Ashley wondered if some of the strain still persisted in him, transmitted through one of the stout peasant girls whom the old Vittorio had taken to his bed in the wild days. His position was obviously one of privilege, since Orgagna, who was brusque with the other servants, was smiling and affectionate in his dealing with the old man.

Here was another mystery.

The dead man was the brother of Elena, and by inference the son of the old steward. How did one explain the bond of friendship between a father and the man who had killed his son? Unless the father, too, were party to the act of murder.

At first blush, it was a crazy thought. Yet the Italians made operas of relationships like that. The ghosts of darker sins haunted the dim palaces of Florence and Venice and the mountain towns. It was an old country, as Harlequin had told him, and its passionate, complex people lived still in the shadow of their turbulent past.

When the meal was over, the others drifted into the house for their siesta; but Ashley, more active and less at ease, wandered down to the shade of the orange garden, where the light was soft on his aching eyes and the air was cool and perfumed.

This time his path led him into a small arbour, set about with stone seats, on the far side of which was a small shrine of the Madonna, an antique statue, set on a small pedestal under a wooden canopy. There was a lamp in front of it and a small vase of flowers, but the oil was spent and the flowers were wilting in the dry summer air.

Ashley sat down on one of the stone benches and looked up at the statue. The tiny face was gentle and remote, set in a timeless tenderness for the Infant cradled in the stiff folds of the cloak. The gilt had weathered off the crown and the blue was long since faded from the robes, but it was still a thing of beauty, of serenity and strange simplicity.

That was another thing you had to reckon with in this people, Ashley remembered. They believed in God. They believed in the Devil. They believed in the Mother of God and in all the ministering hierarchies of saints and angels. Their relationship with the spirit world was real and personal. And if their symbols were florid and their superstitions affronted Puritan tastes, why, they were a frank and lusty people who liked to be able to see their heaven and smell the brimstone of their very baroque hell.

Even men like Orgagna and women like Cosima were nurtured on the same belief. Though they might refuse to practise it, or appear to reject it, they never quite succeeded. It gave their passion a peculiar intensity and their sins a resolute abandon. Risking eternal damnation for love or profit, they were less concerned with the temporal risks of either.

The reflection made him uneasy. He did not belong here. He was a man from the New World, naked, isolated, walking unready among the snares of the old people. He remembered George Harlequin and longed perversely for the comfort of his presence. He was a European. He was attuned to the subtleties of the old ones. He was . . .

Then sleep overtook him and he dozed, slackly, against the rough stone of the garden seat.

He woke to the sound of a woman weeping. He had the presence of mind to make no movement, but sat, tense and silent, watching the pitiful little scene in front of the statue.

Elena Carrese was kneeling there, her head bowed against the rough wood of the pedestal, her shoulders heaving with uncontrollable sobbing. Her hair was in disorder and her hands caressed the feet of the statue. Now and again she raised her head, looking up into the mild eyes of the Madonna, praying passionately in the tumbling dialect of the peninsula. Much of it was lost to Ashley, who spoke good Italian and a little Neapolitan, but by straining and concentrating he pieced out the broken sense of it.

"*Madonna mia!* ... Mother of God! Pity my misery. ... Pity! Pity! I loved him and he has sent me away. I made myself a *putana* for him, damning my soul to hell. Now he wants to marry me to a man who is no man but a *femmenella*—an odd one, who will deny my womanhood and refuse me children. ... Pity me, Madonna! You who are a woman and understand. Pity me and give him back to me! ..."

The words came pouring out, the plea repeated over and over like a refrain, until the grief in her was spent and she crouched, exhausted and despairing, at the foot of the statue.

As he watched her, Ashley understood that now or never he must make her an ally. He knew also that if he made a false move, she would be lost to him for ever. He dared not go near her. He dared not touch her. He spoke to her from where he sat, softly, pityingly, very, very carefully.

"The Madonna understands, little one. I understand, too. I can help you if you let me. I swear to you on the feet of the Madonna that I didn't kill your brother."

Slowly, cautiously, she raised her head and looked at him. Her face was ravaged with tears. There was no sign of the brightly polished beauty who had preened herself on the terrace of the Hotel Caravino. She was

143

back to the beginning again—a peasant girl, broken-hearted, lost and lonely in the big indifferent world. She had no strength to run away. She crouched there, staring at him, with the blank, scared look of a cornered animal.

Ashley sat on the stone seat and smiled at her. He talked rapidly in a low, soothing voice, using as much dialect as he could muster, soothing her as one might soothe a dog, patiently, warily.

"I know what has happened to you, Elena, and I pity you. I know what he's planned for you—and for that I pity you more. I know the lies that have been told you and I know why they were told. They told you I killed your brother. It was not I but others who took him and threw him under the wheels of my car on the road to Sant'Agata. They have told you that I am a liar and a cheat. Yet it is they who have lied. Give me two moments, here, now, and I will tell you the truth and you may judge for yourself. I will try to help you. You need not be afraid of me. If you wish to go, I shall not stop you. If you will sit and talk to me, I shall not touch you nor even come near you. I swear it—on the feet of the Madonna, on the hands of Gesu."

Slowly, ever so slowly, the words began to penetrate the curtain of panic. He watched her become tense, as their meaning came home to her. He saw the blank eyes light with hostility, the hostility give place to fear and curiosity, and faint, faint hope. Then, at long last, she stood up, brushing her knees with a pathetic mechanical gesture, fumbling in her pocket for a handkerchief.

Ashley grinned and tossed her his own.

"Here, use mine! It's bigger."

The handkerchief fell short and fluttered to the ground in front of her. If she picked it up, he would have won. If not . . .

She looked at the handkerchief. She looked at him. She hesitated a moment, then stooped, picked it up, and began wiping the tear stains from her face. Then she walked over and sat down beside him.

"Now tell me," she said flatly. Her face was a wooden mask.

He told her.

He told her everything—his old love for Cosima, his investigation of Orgagna, the drive out to the Retreat, the accident, his interviews with Orgagna and the police. The only thing he did not tell her was his bargain with Tullio Riccioli.

When he had finished, she was sitting like a cataleptic, bolt upright, eyes closed, hands folded in lap. He said, quietly:

"Do you believe me, now?"

Her voice was dead and toneless as she answered him. "Yes."

"Do you understand that we can help each other?"

"Yes."

"I am willing to help you. Will you do the same for me?"

She opened her eyes and looked at him and he saw, with a faint prickling of horror, the new devil he had raised. Elena Carrese was a woman now, eaten up with jealousy, her love soured into a bitter hate for the man who had seduced her first and then shamed her.

"Yes," said Elena Carrese. "Yes, I will help you. I will help you destroy him."

Then, without warning, she buried her face in her hands and wept again, while Ashley patted her shoulder helplessly and tried to soothe her. She leaned to him then, as a child leans to the comforting breast of a parent.

And when Carlo Carrese walked into the arbour he found her in Ashley's arms.

The old man towered above them, his face a wooden mask, his eyes full of cold anger. In one hand he held a short knife and in the other a small posy of flowers he had cut for the shrine. Elena jerked out of Ashley's arms and stared up at him, horrified. Ashley watched him warily, timing his movement in case the old man should strike down at him with the blade.

The old man made no move. His mouth opened and his voice came out, dry and peremptory as the snapping of a stick.

"You, child, go back to the house!"

The girl stood up, edged herself round her father, as if afraid of a blow, then went running swiftly up the path under the orange trees.

Then Carlo Carrese turned on his heel and walked

146

over to the shrine. Methodically, without haste, he emptied the dead flowers, refilled the vase with water and began to arrange the fresh blooms. He reached behind the statue, brought out a small bottle of oil, refilled the lamp and lit it, so that it made a small, weak flickering at the feet of the Madonna. Then he crossed himself, uncovered his head, and stood, with folded hands, a long time in prayer.

Ashley watched him, fascinated. When the old man had finished his prayer, Ashley stood up and walked over to him. He said quietly:

"What were you praying for, Carlo?"

The question surprised him. He considered it for a long moment. Then very deliberately he answered it. All the time his dark, inimical eyes never left Ashley's face.

"When the old Duke died, *signore*, he gave into my hands the care of his son. He made me promise to care for him as if he were my own. I have done that, so far as my strength allowed. Now I am old and have not much strength. So . . . I pray for him . . . and for the honour of his house."

"It is a good prayer, old man," said Ashley calmly.

"I pray for more than that, *signore*." The dark eyes challenged him again. "I pray for the *signora*, who is the wife of my master. I pray that the Madonna may keep her safe—and wise. I pray that soon you will go away from the place and leave us all in peace. I pray for my daughter that she may keep her soul pure to God and her body clean to the man who will marry her."

"Should you not also make another prayer?"

"What?"

"Should you not also pray for your son, who was murdered by your master?"

"I have no son, *signore*."

Then Ashley saw the knife coming up, and the hand, thumb on blade, striking upward towards his belly.

His palm took the impact of the old man's wrist. His fingers closed on it, wrenching and twisting, so that the knife spun away and clattered against the stonework of the seat. He heard the old man gasp with the pain of it and he flung him staggering against the shrine, so that the flowers toppled over and the oil was spilt over the small, tender feet of the Madonna.

"You are a fool, old man," said Ashley breathlessly. "Your master is a cheat and your daughter is lost already. And neither will thank you for what you have done today."

He turned away and walked slowly down through the orange trees. The old man watched him go, with sombre, hating eyes. The little Madonna watched them both. But her eyes were wood and she saw none of it.

CHAPTER NINE

THE SAME NIGHT, after dinner, Orgagna invited Ashley to his study.

They left Cosima and the others at coffee in the *salon* and walked upstairs to a big panelled room that looked out over the water to the humped lights of Capri. The furniture was a florid baroque and two walls were lined with books bound in calf and embossed with the arms of Orgagna. Once again Ashley found himself stifled by so much magnificence, but Orgagna moved among it with the unconscious ease of possession.

He opened a wall cabinet and brought out brandy and cigars. Then, when the brandy was warmed and the cigars were drawing strongly, they sat in great high-backed chairs, facing each other on either side of the window. Orgagna went straight to the point.

"I have decided, Ashley, that it would profit us both to be frank with each other."

"I'd welcome some plain talking."

"Good!" Orgagna fluffed the ash from his cigar and took a careful sip of brandy. "It may surprise you to know that, in spite of what lies between us, I have achieved a—a reluctant respect for you. You have a good brain, much courage and an uncommon strength of purpose. In other circumstances we might have come to friendship. That is now impossible. However, because I respect you, I am able, without too much damage to my pride, to explain myself to you."

"I'm very interested," said Ashley carefully.

"First," said Orgagna, deliberately, "first you should understand that I am aware of your investigations into my personal life and my political and business negotiations. I have followed them with interest from their beginning. I pay you a compliment when I say you have done a very thorough piece of work."

"Thank you."

Orgagna waved aside the irony and went on:

"I know that your principal charges rested finally on a set of letters which you came down here to buy from one Enzo Garofano, since dead. I admit freely that the publication of your story could lose me my seat at the election, and would certainly debar me from accepting a Cabinet appointment. It is, therefore, in my interest to suppress it. You see that I am being quite blunt with you?"

"I see that, yes."

"Your previous association with my wife, her present interest in you, are likewise an embarrassment. Not, you will understand, for reasons of heart, but for reasons of state."

Ashley stirred uneasily in his chair and buried his nose in his brandy-bubble. A flicker of amusement showed in Orgagna's dark eyes.

"Now, Mr. Ashley, we come to the point. I believe that you have in your possession—or at least available to you—the photostats of my letters. I believe that the only thing that prevents their immediate publication is your unfortunate involvement with the police and your state of semi-imprisonment in my house. Is that right?"

Ashley shrugged, indifferently.

"It's a reasonable assumption."

"So . . . !" Organga sat back in his chair and lingered a few moments over the next sip of brandy. "So I find myself in a curious position. I wish to negotiate with you. I know that you are not easily frightened. I do not think you are easily bought. Therefore——" He broke off and waited a few moments, choosing his words with meticulous care. "I propose to do something I have never done in my life before—explain myself! You have interviewed many people on this investigation, Mr. Ashley. You have never questioned me. I think you owe me the right to speak in my own defence, the privilege of a personal explanation. Do you agree?"

"I agree."

"If I convince you, you will withdraw the story?"

"If you convince me—yes. If you don't, I'll publish your explanation in full. Either way you gain something."

"You have a nice sense of justice, Ashley," said Vittorio d'Organga, and there was no irony in the words or in his voice. He got up from his chair and began pacing up and down the room, his footsteps making a soft 'fluff-fluff' on the heavy pile of the carpet. Ashley watched him curiously. Once again he was touched with admiration for the cool strength of the man, his ruthless clarity of judgment, his passionate belief in himself and his own cause. He was under a big strain now. He was sweating under the fans, as the Easterns say. But his dignity was unimpaired. Love him or hate him, exalt him or crucify him, Vittorio d'Orgagna was very much a man.

Suddenly, he stopped pacing and stood leaning back against the big buhl desk, legs crossed, arms akimbo, like an advocate at ease with a good brief. Then he began to talk:

"First, my dear Ashley, I make you a preface—short, simple, without rhetoric or embellishment. This is Italy, not America or England. You must judge me and my actions in my own milieu and with reference to the conditions of my country. It is, I think, an accepted principle. A murder in Chicago is a criminal offence. In Africa it may be a religious act, a ritual of worship. Do I make myself clear?"

"Yes."

"Do you accept the principle?"

"Subject to interpretation."

Orgagna smiled at him with grudging approval.

"Neatly taken, my friend. For the present that is all I ask. Now, I told you I am aware of the charges you make against me. There are three principal ones: first, that I procured a loan from this Government, out of dollar relief funds, to found an industry in the depressed South and that I then diverted these funds to my factories in the North. Second, that being charged with the distribution of American grain-seed to peasant farmers in distressed areas, I made the distribution only to members of my party and also caused them to pay for it. Thirdly, that, in contravention of the laws of Italy, I have exported funds and held them in reserve in American banks. Is that a just summary of your case, Ashley?"

"Yes."

"What are you expecting me to do? Deny it?"

"I don't see how you can."

"I don't deny it, Mr. Ashley!" The words came out sharp and clear as a whip-crack. "It is true—all of it! And there is more yet, that even your careful investigation has not uncovered."

"At least you're frank about it," Ashley grinned at him over the lip of his glass.

"It is illegal, all of it," Orgagna went on calmly. "Yet I claim that all of it was necessary and justified. I know what you are saying to yourself. Every criminal justifies his own acts. Even the Devil has scripture on the tip of his tongue. You are wrong, my friend, grievously wrong."

"I've suspended judgment," said Ashley calmly. "I am waiting to hear the defence."

Orgagna thrust himself forward from the desk and walked slowly across the room to stand looking out to the lights of the siren island and the silver track of the moon across the soft water. He was a man caught up to visions—of mystery and terror and greatness and implacable judgment. The soft light picked out the fine patrician bones of his face and deepened the brooding shadows about his mouth. Slowly he turned back to face Ashley. The lights were at his back now and his face was all in shadow. Ashley could not say whether he smiled or frowned, but his voice was vibrant with conviction.

"You, Ashley, are a man from a new world. Because of your abundant riches, you have reached, quickly, a high stage of technical evolution. Your workers have automobiles and your women have their children in aseptic hospitals instead of being wrenched to parturition by ignorant midwives. Your sons have room to grow and your daughters have men to marry. You have made a new history. You need no longer carry the burdens of the old. We—my people—have not those things. Here in the South, particularly, we have illiteracy, unemployment, poor communications, meagre resources. To change this state of affairs needs vision and enterprise—not the vision of the bureaucrats and the party men, not the enterprise of the place-hunter. It needs men with boldness and vision, prepared, if necessary, to step outside the framework of the law to do what must be done. You ask me why I diverted funds from the South to the North? First, they could only be got by a lie. Second, if I tried to start business here, in the South, without supplies, without communications, without trained operatives, we'd lose the money, pour it down the bottomless sewer, to no profit. In the North it will employ two thousand men. It will return profit to the country as a whole. It will pay taxes to build schools in Naples. It will attract more money —investment money from your country, because you are bankers and not a charitable organisation. And that is how it should be.

"You say to me, why did I sell the grain which was given as a gift—and then only to party members? I will answer that, too. We are an ignorant people. Our peasants are stubborn, sunk in old superstition, mistrustful, unwilling to organise themselves; so that the land becomes fruitless and trees die and the bloodlines are ruined. To give them a gift is to waste it—or to watch them sell it in their turn, while they laugh at you in their sleeves. Make them buy it, and they value it. Confine it to the party and you teach them the value of co-operation and improvement. It is wrong. It is illegal. But do you justify folly just because it does not contravene the law?

"Think of it thus, Ashley! Forget me! Forget that I am the husband of a woman you love! Look at the real things, the situation as it exists. Ask yourself, if, sitting in my place, you would have done otherwise.

"Finally you ask about my funds in America. I will tell you that when I want machinery, machine-tools, raw materials to keep the factory working and the workers eating, I must go to a bureaucrat in Rome, who cuts my dollar allocation in half with the stroke of a pen. He knows nothing! He sits at his coffee-table on the pavement and puffs out his chest at the pretty girls. He doesn't see the hunger in the back streets and the children blotched with pellagra. The law is on his side, ancient laws that have never been changed since Justinian. But I say, humanity and wisdom is on mine!" He sat down heavily in his chair and passed a slim hand wearily across his forehead. "There is my defence, Ashley. You know enough to weigh it for yourself. If there is any question you would like to ask me, I shall try to answer it, honestly."

"There's only one," said Ashley quietly.

"Ask it."

"Why did you have Garofano murdered?"

"I didn't," said Orgagna bleakly.

And Ashley was half-convinced that he spoke the truth.

Then, for a long time, it seemed, they faced each other across a pool of silence—a dark, shadowy pool, stirred by uneasy ripples of doubt and suspicion.

Finally Ashley spoke and his words were slow stones counted into the silent, stirring water:

"I've heard your defence—with interest and a certain sympathy. I'm still reserving judgment. But I must know this first. Who killed Garofano? Who checked my movements with Cosima and had him flung under the wheels of the car?"

"I can't tell you that."

Orgagna's face was still in shadow and Ashley had the queer impression that his voice was disembodied, separate and remote from the figure in the opposite chair.

"You mean you won't."

"As you wish."

Then Ashley flung it at him, harsh and high-pitched.

"I'll tell you then! It was Carlo Carrese, steward of your house!"

There was no reaction from the shadowy figure opposite. There was a pause, and then the polite, remote voice asked him:

"What makes you say that, Mr. Ashley?"

"He tried to kill me this afternoon."

Then the reaction came—a long, sighing exhalation of breath ending in a round "Oh" of surprise. Then Orgagna got up from his chair and walked over to the window. Ashley could not see his face but the question came to him clearly.

"Do you mind telling me how and where?"

Ashley told him. Orgagna stood staring out the window, a dark, motionless figure against the moonlight and the strung lights of the distant island. When the terse and vivid little narrative was finished, he turned back to Ashley. He was smiling, a little crookedly, and there were lines of weariness on his dark, fine features. He said, simply:

"Let's have another brandy, shall we?"

"Sure."

Ashley got up, walked across the room and stood with Orgagna at the polite little ceremony of the drinks.

"*Salute!*"

"*Salute!*"

They drank, ritually. Orgagna put down his glass and mopped his face and his hands with a silk handkerchief. Truly, he was sweating under the fans, but his voice was still under control, quiet and reasonable.

"I think I should tell you about Carlo Carrese."

"Yes?"

"He was, as he told you, my father's steward. It has always been a family joke that there was Orgagna blood in him, too. Remembering our history . . ." Orgagna smiled, wearily, ". . . I think it is quite possible. Be that as it may, there has always been a bond between us. He has always been a good and loyal steward of the estates and when my father died he gave me the love that he might have spent on his own son, if he had had one."

"He did have one," said Ashley bluntly. "Enzo Garofano."

Orgagna looked at him sharply. Then his face relaxed into a smile and he shook his head.

"No! Garofano was not his son. Garofano was the son of his wife by another man. Had you known a little more about us, you would have guessed from the name. It is not a family name at all. It is the name of a flower which in English is called carnation. He was born in the spring-time, you see, in the time of the carnations, and because his father had gone long since his mother gave him that name."

"Where was Carlo all this time?"

"In Milan with my father, who was then founding our business."

"Oh!"

"When Carlo came home, he followed the custom of our people—which has much to recommend it. He thrashed his wife and then forgave her, and thrashed her periodically to remind her of her folly. The baby was boarded out to a wet-nurse in Sant' Agata, and later adopted. Then, Elena was born, and one day her mother introduced her to her half-brother. As children do, she became attached to him, and in spite of the antagonism of Carlo, the boy used to come here and play. The mother died early. I—I paid for his education. I never liked him, but for Elena's sake, I was prepared to let him come here to visit her. Carlo, of course, hated him. But . . ." Orgagna shrugged and made a wry mouth, ". . . because he is a good servant, he bowed to the wishes of the master."

"Is that why he killed Garofano?"

Orgagna looked at him with blank eyes and shook his head, slowly.

"I have not said that Carlo killed him. You said it. I have given you this information for a very simple reason."

"Which is?"

"To explain to you that Carlo Carrese is a member of

our family. What touches him, touches me. He is an old man, Ashley. The burden of his years is heavy on him, and the family of Orgagna is still in his debt. The only way I can pay the debt is to protect him and give him a comfortable old age. I shall do that, even if . . ."

He broke off and the unspoken threat hung like a suspended discord between them.

"Say it, Orgagna," said Ashley sharply.

Orgagna shook his head.

"No, my friend, no. It would sound too much like a threat and tonight of all nights I must avoid that impression. I am the accused. I am pleading my case. This . . . this story of Carrese and his wife's son is an irrelevance, which we may discuss later."

It was so subtly and so blandly done that Ashley almost missed it. Orgagna had intrigued him with talk of a bargain. He had flattered him with sympathy and seduced him with heady rhetoric. Now he was explaining the nice balance of forces: 'you have the photostats and the means to publish them; I have the power to convict you of murder, which I have planned and which an old retainer has executed. I think you would like to be quit of this story. Now let us see if we can arrange a formula which salves your conscience and shows you a profit. . . .'

Ashley remembered the final warning of George Harlequin and waited uneasily while His Excellency explained himself further. He did it with gravity and surprising force.

"It is an old illusion, Ashley, that good men make good rulers—that human beings can be governed with faith, hope and charity and a set of Papal encyclicals. The function of government is to provide a strong, secure framework within which people may live and evolve slowly to a better way of life. The virtue of the ruler has nothing to do with it. It is his strength which matters, his wisdom and his capacity for turning the corruption and the weakness of his fellows to the profit of the body politic. Progress demands security. Security is founded on strength. I am not a good man—far from it. But I am a strong one. I have skill in politics. I have strong, financial influence. Given the chance, I can hold this country together for five years at least—long enough to strengthen the foundations of public order and set the wheels of progress turning. Without me, the weak alliance of Left and Right is destroyed and we are back to division, discontent and economic chaos. It is strange, very strange, that the power to make or to destroy should rest at this moment in the hands of a man like yourself, a spectator, whose sole financial holding is his monthly pay-cheque, whose only stake in this country is his passion for another man's wife."

Ashley flushed angrily. Orgagna was fighting in earnest now. The buttons were off and the points were probing closer and closer to the bone.

Orgagna shifted ground. His voice changed. He questioned softly, with sympathy and a touch of pathos.

"What do you want, Ashley? What drives you to

this? What is it that makes you gamble so wildly to print a story that, three weeks later, will be brushed off the front pages to make room for a film star's wedding or an aeroplane crash in America? What do you get out of it that matches the misery you will cause? Is it money? I doubt it. Is it satisfaction to your vanity, to your desire for power? Is it the blind zeal of the crusader? Believe me, I want to understand."

Ashley looked up.

"You're putting me in the witness-box now."

Orgagna nodded.

"The defence, too, has the right to cross-examine."

"Fair enough."

Ashley took out a cigarette, tapped it, thoughtfully, on his thumb-nail, lit it and watched the first slow spirals of smoke climb upward towards the shadows of the ceiling. He, too, was on trial and he knew it. In a curious sense, his profession was on trial. And he knew that unless he could justify himself to himself, he could never sleep soundly again. He would have to join the cynics who did their job for bread, butter and a bonus, and be damned to the rest of it. Hesitantly at first, but gaining slowly in power and conviction, he, too, began to speak:

"You ask me my motives, Orgagna. I'd be a liar if I said they were less tangled or more worthy than anyone else's. Money? Yes. I'll get paid enough for this story to leave me comfortably fixed for a year or two. I'll make a reputation that will put me at the top of my profession and enable me to command more money. Vanity? Yes, that too. You can't adopt a profession if you don't have a pride. Pride feeds on success. The greed of power? I doubt it—unless there's a perverted sense of power in the irresponsible detachment of the observer. Jealousy of you and of Cosima? No. I lost her long ago. I was never bitter enough to make a vendetta out of it."

"But you're still in love with her, as she is with you?"

"The question's irrelevant," said Ashley baldly.

"Strike it from the record," said Orgagna coolly. "Please go on."

"Every profession has its cynics and its profiteers. There are men with the power of healing in their hands who use it to kill the unborn or do mammary plastics on declining dowagers. There are judges who pervert justice and priests who pervert the gospel. There are also newsmen, big and small, who prostitute themselves in the twin temples of Policy and Circulation. But most of them, in their stumbling, purblind fashion, still believe that their function is to communicate the truth. They don't own the channels of communication. They are forced quite often to shifts and stratagems to get the truth into print. Often they can't print the whole truth, but they still believe in the right of the people to know the whole truth. They believe that the truth has a virtue of its own, a fruitfulness of its own, and that to stifle or distort it is to kill a source of life and destroy a promise of improvement. Tyranny flourishes in dark cellars.

Corruption breeds in closed councils. And if a child dies of tuberculosis, as I have seen them die in the *bassi* of Naples, it is because the truth was hidden or told too late. That's why I'm printing this story, Orgagna. Because the people have the right to know about you, before they put their future in your hands."

A long tube of ash dropped from his cigarette and fell soundlessly on the carpet. He made a little gesture of apology and stubbed out the butt in a silver ash-tray.

"That's the motive, Orgagna, as clear as I can make it. I admit the others too, but I think that's the real one, the strongest of all. If I didn't believe that, I'd hold you up here and now for a fat price, take Cosima with me and leave on the first plane from Rome to grow oranges in California."

"It might be cheap at the price," said Orgagna smoothly. "How much?"

"No deal," said Ashley.

"Will you sell me the photostats and print the rest of the story?"

"No."

"Will you think it over for a day or two?"

"It won't make any difference."

Orgagna looked at him with a thin, subtle smile.

"Wisdom is a slow growth, my friend, and I have learned to be patient. Think it over. Sleep on it."

He held out his hand.

"Good-night, Ashley, *sogni d'oro*! Golden dreams!"

164

CHAPTER TEN

THE MOONLIGHT flowed in through the windows
of his bedroom and lay in soft pools among the rose-
petals on the floor. The heavy carved furniture made
grotesque shadows in the angles of the room. The
cherubs on the coffered ceiling were hidden in the high
darkness. And Richard Ashley lay wakeful on the big
four-poster bed, pondering his first day in the Villa
Orgagna.

There was profit and there was loss. The profit was
in the new information he had gathered—the connection of the dead man with the Orgagna family; the
rejection of Elena by Orgagna, her jealousy and despair;
the knowledge that Tullio Riccioli could be bought;
and that Cosima had not sold him out, but had lied to
protect him; the fact that Orgagna feared him enough
to attempt a bargain.

The loss was less apparent, but more serious. There
was now an open breach between himself and Orgagna.
Orgagna would know, as he knew himself, that the
stalemate could not last indefinitely. One or other
must be destroyed in the end. His own safety depended
on a lie. Orgagna believed he had the photostats. He
could not fight too long from such slippery ground.

He must either find the photostats or get himself out of Orgagna's hands.

The only person who might give him a clue to their location was Elena Carrese; but after the episode at the shrine, he thought that communication between them might be made more and more difficult.

He stared up into the shadows and thought about Elena Carrese. A woman scorned, a woman of the South to boot, her first impulse would be to revenge herself on the man who had wronged her. The weapons lay ready enough to her hands. As Orgagna's secretary, she would know the contents of the files. She would know, too, the progress of Ashley's own investigation. She would see clearly enough how to strike at Orgagna. She might reason further, to the financial profit which could free her from marriage to Tullio Riccioli and give her a dowry to marry a man of her choice.

She could take the letters from the files, pass them to her half-brother for photostatting and sale, then sit back and wait for the ruin of Orgagna. And all the while her little peasant soul would be torn between love and hatred for him, between despair and tenuous hope.

The hope would die, gradually, painfully, as she saw the ganglia of Orgagna's information service reach out to touch the informer. She would know of the telephone calls from Rome to Naples and Sorrento and the Villa Orgagna, as His Excellency's agents reported the movements and contacts of Garofano. She would know of the new, big offer tempting him closer to

Orgagna's hands. She would warn him, but he would not listen, for venality is a besetting sin of these poverty-stricken people.

And when at last the hands closed round him, she would not know for certain who had killed him. She would not dare to know, because then her lover must be damned as a murderer, her father, too, perhaps. So for safety, she would settle the guilt on Ashley himself —the ignorant executioner.

The more he thought on it, the closer he came to the conviction that this was the truth. He thought that even Captain Granforte might accept it, given the letters in his soft insinuating hands.

Given the letters. . . .

When they had talked at the hotel, Garofano had said they were close at hand—available if the price were met. Ashley thought that was probably the truth. Otherwise he would not have come to the interview. That meant they were somewhere in Sorrento, lodged in the bank perhaps, or with a trusted friend—except that informers had no friends and trusted no one.

Then a new thought came to him, but before he had time to pursue it, the door of his room opened softly and Cosima came in.

She was dressed for bed. She wore a dressing-gown of quilted satin. Her hair was caught back from her face and tied with a bow behind her neck. Her feet were soundless in soft, Florentine mules. She carried a towel and a bowl of water and a small flask of oil.

Ashley sat up in bed and looked at her in amazement.

"Cosima! Are you crazy?"

"Your eyes, Richard. I saw them at dinner. They're scarred and inflamed. I—I thought the least I could do was . . . this."

She walked to the windows and drew the heavy curtains, switched on the lights and set the things down on the bedside-table. Ashley watched her, wondering and cautious. When she came close to him, he made no move to touch her, but lay back on the pillows while she bathed his eyes carefully and dressed the inflamed tissues. Her hands were soft on his skin and her voice was gentle and regretful.

"In that moment, Richard, I came as close as I have ever done to hating you. I could not understand that you should harbour thoughts like that against me. I could not believe that you could kiss me and hold me in your arms and turn something beautiful into a horrible lie. No, no! Don't try to talk. Lie still and let me finish. Your eyes are terribly sore. Later, when I began to think about it, I understood how it must have looked to you: that I had lent myself to a plan to destroy you and save my husband. I—I don't blame you now. I blame myself that I did not speak out and . . ."

"I don't blame you, either. On the beach I was trying to tell you I was sorry." He chuckled grimly. "Only you wouldn't let me finish. Will you kiss me now?"

She kissed him lightly on the lips and bent again to the last bathing of his eyes with the soothing oil. She wiped his cheeks and forehead with the towel, laid it on the bedside-table and sat down on the edge of the bed. He drew her down and kissed her again, but after a moment she disengaged herself and looked down at him with tender, troubled eyes.

"Richard . . . what's going to happen to us?"

"What do you mean?"

"After what has happened, I cannot go on living with my husband. I doubt whether he would want it, anyway. Once the elections are over, I shall be of no further use to him."

"Divorce?"

"Italian law does not permit it."

"We could go away. You could divorce him in another country."

"Yes."

There was no conviction in her voice. Only the flat admission of a known fact.

"You're a Catholic, is that it? The Church condemns divorce and the remarriage of divorced persons."

"I—I have lived so long away from the Church, I suppose it makes no difference what I do now."

"I don't belong to the Church, Cosima. It makes no difference to me how we're married or by whom. I can understand that it might make a difference to you. Would you be happy that way?"

"Happy?" She looked away from him and began twisting the rings on her finger. "I don't know what happiness means, Richard. In the old days, I thought I was happy with you. I found it wasn't enough. I thought I would be happier with what Orgagna could give. That wasn't enough either. Now . . . I don't know. Perhaps it is never enough."

Ashley looked at her, puzzled.

"What are you trying to tell me, Cosima? That you don't love me?"

"How can you say that?"

"I'm not saying it. I'm asking you. Do you want me to take you away and marry you? I'm willing to do it, provided it makes you happy. Do you want to leave your husband and live with me, without benefit of clergy? We can do that, too, though there's not much profit in it for either of us. There's only one thing I can't do, sweetheart."

"What's that?"

"Come to terms with your conscience. No lover in the world can do that, and we're both old enough to know it. I'm afraid it's up to you, Cosima. *Barkis is willin'.*"

"What does that mean?"

He grinned and ran his hands through his cropped hair.

"It's an English phrase. It means you've got a bridegroom, but it's the bride's privilege to name the day."

She was silent a moment. She looked down at her hands, twisting the rings upward on her finger so that he could see the indentations where they had worked themselves into the white skin.

"Richard, there's something I want to say."

"Say it."

"I—I think we could be happy together. I think, perhaps, the Church will not miss one stray soul who has wandered a long way already. But there is one thing I cannot do. I cannot build my happiness on the ruin of a man who, after all, is my husband, and who, for all his ruthlessness, has been kind to me. That, it seems to me, would be a sort of final denial of the little good that is left in me."

"Up on the mountain you told me to print the story,"

"I know . . . I know." Her voice was low and miserable. "Up on the mountain, I was drunk with the joy of meeting you, with the taste of—of something I had given up as lost. I know now that it was an illusion. I cannot do it. I will marry you, Richard. I will live with you, whichever is open to us. But I want you to give up this story. I want you to suppress it, kill it. You have reason enough, God knows. Then, I think, there might be a chance for both of us."

And there it was, bald and breath-taking, the same bargain that Orgagna had put to him an hour before. They would sell anything, these people—their souls, their bodies, the folk who loved them—to preserve the last shreds of outworn honour. He looked at her with loathing and disgust and she shrank back, as if from a blow.

"Get out! Go back to your husband! Tell him I liked the proposition better when he gave it to me himself. Tell him I'm not interested. I can buy it cheaper in the back streets of Naples, where at least the girls are honest!"

Wide-eyed and horror-stricken, Cosima stared at him. The colour drained from her face and the hand that she held to her lips trembled as if with the ague. Her voice was a terrified whisper.

"You ... you say that ..."

"In God's name, get out!"

Slowly, like a woman in a trance, she gathered up her things from the table and walked away. Half-way to the door she turned and looked at him. Her face was tragic. Her voice was steady but full of heart-breaking grief.

"I am sorry for you, Richard. I am more sorry for you than I am for myself. You are so eaten up with pride that you cannot see the truth when it is thrust under your nose. Nothing will stand in your way. Not love, nor pity, nor—nor even death. Your fine words are a mockery. Your big story is a sham because you proclaim truth to feed your ambition and clamour for justice to feed the hate in your heart. God help you, Richard. Nobody else can!"

She turned away, a bowed, defeated figure. The door closed behind her like the door of a lost paradise from which he was now shut out eternally. He switched off the lights and lay staring up into the darkness. He knew now that he must finish the story at whatever cost, though the taste of it would be like ashes on his tongue. After a while, he fell asleep, tossing and muttering, tumbling the bed into disorder, winding the sheets about him like a shroud.

Sometime after midnight, he woke, sweating and startled. He sat up. The room was dark and quiet as a tomb, but his whole body was prickling with fear.

Then he heard it: a soft, muffled scratching, like a mouse skittering in the wainscot. He called softly:

"Who's there?"

The sound stopped. He reached up to the light-cord, pressed the switch. The room was flooded with light, dazzling him. He blinked and looked about him. The room was empty. The curtains hung, heavy and unstirring over the casements. He looked at the door.

Lying in front of it was a brown manila envelope. The sound he had heard was the noise of it being thrust under the edge of the door and along the tiles. He leapt out of bed and picked up the envelope.

When he opened it, the contents slid out into his hand —six photostat copies of the Orgagna letters!

For a long moment he stared at them, hardly understanding his good fortune. The big story was complete. With the evidence he had gathered at the Villa Orgagna, he could convince Captain Granforte of his own innocence and of the involvement of Orgagna and his household in the death of Garofano. If the Captain proved difficult, he could demand to be taken into custody pending the arrival of the American Consul. Tomorrow the triumph would be complete. Tomorrow...! He remembered that there were hours of the night and the day to pass before he could communicate with Sorrento and have himself removed from the Villa Orgagna. Until then, he must find a safe hiding-place for the photostats. To carry them on his person would be a needless risk.

He set the chain-bolt on the door so that no one could enter from the passage. He went to the windows and closed them, locking them carefully and drawing the heavy curtains. Then he looked about the room.

There was enough furniture in it to fill a small hotel, but none of it was safe from dusting and cleaning and from the prying fingers of the servants—curious as jackdaws about the possessions of a foreign visitor. The mattress was a classic hiding-place, of course. But a tear in the ticking would show and anything unusual might be reported to the major-domo, Carlo Carrese.

Then his eyes fell on the old Florentine bridal chest, with its ornate carvings and its heavy worm-pocked wood. It sat flush on the floor. He doubted if it had been moved in years. He walked over to it, bent down and heaved up one corner with his shoulder. It was heavy as iron, but it lifted a finger's height and he saw that the tiles underneath were covered with dust and fluff. Good enough. He slipped the envelope underneath and lowered the corner of the chest. A small cloud of dust fluffed out. He wiped it up carefully with his handkerchief.

It was done. The photostats were safe against casual search.

Now he might address himself to the question of where they had come from and why.

The answer seemed obvious enough—Elena Carrese. She had promised to ally herself with him. She had handed over the photostats as evidence of good faith. More than this, their safety must have been jeopardised by the happenings in the orange-arbour in front of the shrine. Her father would suspect her of collusion with the foreigner. Orgagna would take it as a certainty. There was sound reason for getting them out of her possession as soon as possible.

How had she come by them in the first place? That, too, was ridiculously simple, now he knew more about her relationship with Garofano. The little informer would have come to the hotel early, well before the time of his appointment. He would have delivered the photostats to Elena to hold for him until after the bargaining.

When the bargaining failed and he had taken himself off, he would not have been too much concerned. The material was in safe hands. He could return and collect it at a less embarrassing time. But he had never come back. Why? Ashley knew that if he could answer that question, the chain of evidence against Orgagna and Carrese would be complete. What had happened to Garofano between the time he left the hotel and the moment when he was tossed out into space and under the wheels of a speeding car?

Granforte might find the answer to that if he set his

boys digging about Sorrento, questioning this one and that, checking times and movements. Ashley smiled to himself at the thought of the moon-faced Captain sorting out the embarrassing evidence and regretting the promotion he would never get.

After a while, sleep claimed him and whirled him off into a nightmare in which he stood alone in the middle of a sunlit desert and heard Cosima crying out for him. But whichever way he turned, he could not see her, because she was lost to him for ever.

He woke early, haggard and unrefreshed. His body ached and his skin was slack and dry. When he opened the curtains, the raw sunlight hurt his eyes. His tongue was coated and bitter in his mouth.

He shaved quickly, slipped into trunks and a dressing-gown and headed down to the beach for a swim.

The air was still fresh and the orange leaves were shining with dew. There was the smell of the earth and the piping of the morning birds and the distant, rhythmic clouting of an axe on wood.

As he broke out from the olive-groves on to the grass of the cliff-top, he saw a man standing near the rock where the old shepherd had sat the day before. He wore rough, peasant clothes and carried a double-barrelled shot-gun.

Ashley saluted him and called a greeting:

"*Buon giorno! Cosa fai?* What are you doing?"

"*Quaglie!*" came the shouted answer. "Quail!"

Ashley stopped in his tracks and looked at him. The

quail came in the spring and were soon shot out. This was high summer. He called:

"Isn't it late for quail?"

The fellow shrugged and gestured and turned away. So far as he was concerned the conversation was over. Ashley turned down on to the shaly path that led to the beach.

The first plunge shocked the sleep out of him and he swam steadily out into the deep, where the water was blue as sapphire over the ribs of Roman galleys and the coral bones of Phœnician sailormen. The salt stung his damaged eyes and, after a while, he turned on his back and floated, shutting his lids against the glare, and feeling the sun dry his chest and his belly, while the cool water still lapped about the rest of him.

It was a good time, a pleasant time. He began to feel clean again, as if the waters were washing away the grime from his spirit as they cleansed his skin of night-sweat and fatigue. An illusion, of course, like so many other things, but it pleased him to cherish it for these brief suspended moments between the empty sky and the sea-floor full of the detritus of the centuries.

Then the tide began to shift, running swiftly out between Capri and the point of the Sorrentine peninsula. He rolled himself over in the water and headed back to shore.

As he was towelling himself, he glanced up at the cliff-top. The hunter of quail was there, standing black and motionless against the blue sky, the gun cradled in the crook of his arm.

Ashley put on his dressing-gown and walked thoughtfully to the house.

When he had dressed, he went down on to the terrace and a servant brought him coffee and fresh rolls and a bowl of fruit. The others, she told him, were taking breakfast in their rooms. He thought he detected a faint disapproval of crazy *forestieri* who stirred too early before the household had time to rub the sleep out of its eyes and set itself in order for the day.

He finished his coffee, smoked a leisurely cigarette and decided to treat himself to a walk around the property. It seemed quite likely to be his last opportunity. He stepped off the terrace, crossed the lawn and began following a path that led up the hillside, away from the sea-reaches.

The lower slope was planted with oranges and olives, but beyond them, where the slope was steeper and the ground rougher, the land was terraced and planted with vines. Beyond the vines were the silos and the storehouses huddled against the high stone wall, which was the boundary of the property. His eyes followed the line of the wall and he saw with mild surprise that it stopped short on the edge of a humped escarpment. Then he realised that the escarpment was the cutting of the road—the same road on which Cosima and he had driven up to Il Deserto, on which Enzo Garofano had been killed.

178

He quickened his steps. This was important. If he could show that the spot from which Garofano had been flung was part of the Orgagna property . . . He gasped with surprise and stumbled backward as a man rose up from the vines in front of him.

He, too, was a peasant. Like the other he carried a shot-gun. Ashley twisted his features into the semblance of a smile and greeted him as he had greeted the other.

"Good-morning. You startled me. What are you doing?"

"*Quaglie, signore,*" said the fellow succinctly.

Ashley grinned at him and shook his head.

"You're wasting your time. There are no quail now. Spring is a long time gone and the other hunters have shot them out."

The peasant stared at him with stubborn, hostile eyes.

"There are still some birds."

"*Come vuoi,*" said Ashley indifferently. "Have it your own way."

He stuck his hands in his pockets and began to walk up the path towards the wall. The peasant stepped out in front of him.

"Not that way, *signore.*"

"Why not?"

"You will frighten the birds."

"To hell with the . . ."

But he didn't finish it. The gun was pointed at his chest. The peasant grinned shiftily and licked his lips.

His stubby finger curled around the trigger. Ashley turned and walked slowly back the way he had come.

Let Granforte look for his own evidence. The big story was still a long way from the teleprinters and he couldn't get it there with a charge of birdshot in his chest.

When he reached the shelter of the trees, he looked back. The peasant had left the path and was beginning to patrol the stone wall from the far end, down towards the cutting. On the lip of the cutting there was another man; two hundred yards below him, another. Each carried a gun, and if there were birds to be shot, they didn't seem to care. They were all looking down towards the olive trees, where a tall American in a bright sun-shirt stood leaning against a gnarled grey trunk.

'Like a sitting duck,' thought Ashley. A squawking silly duck who didn't know what time of day it was.

He looked at his watch. Nine-fifteen. Captain Granforte should be in his office by now. Best to telephone him and have done with this sinister little comedy before somebody got hurt.

He trod out his cigarette and headed down towards the house. The hunters on the hill whistled to each other and made derisive gestures as they watched the flicker of his coloured shirt in and out among the tree-trunks.

The terrace was still deserted. He crossed it swiftly and walked into the *salon* where the telephone was. A thick-bodied peasant with broken shoes and a patched dress was washing down the tiled floor. She looked up at him a moment, then resumed her patient, back-breaking task.

Ashley picked up the telephone. There was no dial tone but he knew that Italian phones were apt to be temperamental. He jiggled the cradle a few times, then tried to dial the exchange. The line was still dead. He thought it would probably be dead for some time.

He thought also that the moment had come to do business with Tullio Riccioli.

CHAPTER ELEVEN

IT WAS WELL AFTER TEN before Tullio showed up. He came out on to the terrace, wearing only black trunks and a pair of espadrilles and carrying his artist's gear under his arm. His smooth brown body shone with health and he walked with the swaying, conscious grace of a preening peacock.

Ashley greeted him casually and waited until he had set up his easel and begun work on the unfinished canvas. Then, without haste, he got up and walked across to him. He said quietly:

"Keep working, Tullio. If anyone comes, I'm talking to you about the picture."

"*D'accordo!*" Riccioli gave him a swift, sidelong look and went on with his work. "What do you want to talk about?"

"I want you to do a job for me—today."

"Do I get paid?"

"Surely."

"How much?"

"Five hundred dollars in advance and another five hundred at the end of it."

"It sounds important."

"It is—to me."

"What's the job?"

"I want you to go down to Sorrento and deliver a message to the Englishman, George Harlequin."

"What's the message?"

"Just tell him I have what he wants and I'd like to see him here as soon as possible."

Tullio stepped back from the easel and surveyed his work with theatrical care.

"Is there anything else?"

"No. Just deliver the message. Can you get away?"

"No reason why not. I'd like a change anyway. This place is like a museum."

"How soon can you leave?"

"Before lunch. I'll have to ask Orgagna for the car. I'm not going to tramp around in this heat. Er—when do I collect the advance?"

"Come to my room when you go in. I'll give it to you then."

"Very well."

And that was the end of it. Tullio went back to work and Ashley strolled back to his chair under the big coloured umbrella. He would have preferred to go back to the beach and spend the morning bathing and baking in the sun, but he thought better of it. The folk of the peninsula were chancy and temperamental. There were too many chances of accident, when they went shooting quail out of season.

Tullio Riccioli was chancy, too, of course. Capricious, self-absorbed, venal, void of love and incapable of loyalty, he made a dangerous ally. He and his kind haunted the international resorts, picking up a modest living from foolish dowagers and wealthy inverts. They were up to all the tricks of their ancient trade—blackmail, minor cruelty and theft from those who lacked the courage to speak out against them. Their talents ran to early seed and, once their youth was over, their vices impoverished them quickly. But they were all susceptible to one lure—easy money, the crackle of hard currency in their slim pampered hands. Ashley hoped fervently that with five hundred dollars still to collect Tullio's loyalty would last the short distance to Sorrento and back. But he knew that he could not be sure of it.

The next member of the household to come on to the terrace was Elena Carrese. In spite of the heat, she was dressed in a bright peasant skirt, an embroidered vest and a blouse buttoned to the wrists. Tullio gave her a curt nod and went on with his painting. Ashley called to her cheerfully, and, after a moment's hesitation, she came over and sat beside him.

She was calmer this morning, he noticed. Her hands were steady and her face was composed. But resentment still smouldered in her dark eyes and the skin of her face was tight and strained under the make-up. Ashley offered her a cigarette and lit it for her. She smoked a few moments in silence, then, in a low voice, she said:

"Did you get what I sent you?"

"Yes, thank you. Do you want to talk about it now?"

"No. Just keep them safe. For your sake and mine."

He looked at her sharply, but her face was turned away from him and she was staring out across the garden.

"Why do you say that? Are you afraid of something?"

"Afraid?" She gave a bitter laugh. "Not now! Not ever again."

"What—what happened yesterday . . . after you left me?"

In a flat, expressionless voice, she told him.

"My father beat me. He beat me like a barefoot farm-girl from the mountains. That's why I'm dressed like this, to hide the bruises. He called me a *putana* and worse, because he found me in your arms under the orange trees. He threatened to kill me if I ever came near you again. But I laughed in his face and he beat me again as he used to beat my mother—until he was tired and had to let me go. I wonder . . ." She puffed nervously at the cigarette. ". . . I wonder what he would say if he knew about Vittorio and me."

Ashley gaped at her in amazement.

"Doesn't he know already?"

She laughed again, a dry, unhappy little sound, incongruous from her young lips.

"How could he? We have never been together in this house. To him, Vittorio is the *gran' signore* who has taken a little peasant girl and made her a *signora* out of

185

the goodness of his heart; and who now completes the charity by marrying her to a suitable husband."

"God Almighty!" Ashley swore in English.

Elena went on bitterly:

"My father is a simple man, as you see. He believes in God and the house of Orgagna. He believes that there are three sorts of women—virgins, wives and the others. He beats me to see that I stay in the class to which God and His Excellency have called me."

"What would happen if he found out the truth?"

"I don't know," said Elena Carrese sombrely. "I think it would be the end of the world for him."

"Do you love him?"

"No. I—I am fond of him in a certain way. But I have never loved him as I loved my mother. He never belonged to us, you see. He belonged to the house of Orgagna."

"Do you know he tried to kill me in the garden yesterday?"

She nodded slowly.

"Yes. He told me that while he was beating me. He told me he had failed once and that he would not fail again. When he is angry, he is a little mad, I think."

Then he put it to her, softly, soberly, the last damning question:

"Do you know he killed your brother?"

She swung round to face him. Her mouth drooped slackly. Her eyes were wide with shock. She got the words out with difficulty.

"Do—do you mean that?"

Ashley laid a firm hand on her wrist to steady her. He dared not risk a scene on the open terrace, in full view of the windows, with Tullio Riccioli only a dozen yards away. He spoke, swiftly and urgently.

"Try to control yourself. Don't let anybody see that you are disturbed."

Her whole body stiffened and she held herself rigid and tense, trying to steady herself. She said quickly:

"I—I won't do anything stupid. Just tell me."

Ashley hurried into his explanation. At any moment now, Orgagna or Cosima might come out on to the terrace and the opportunity would be lost to him.

"I can't prove it, you understand, but I believe it's true. I believe that Orgagna warned your father that Garofano had the photostats in his possession. Somebody from this house paid Roberto at the hotel to telephone my movements with Cosima. I believe that when your brother walked out, after our quarrel, he was met by someone who bundled him into a car and drove him up here to the villa. They probably searched him for the photostats. Then, when they didn't find them, I think they took him to the edge of the cutting and waited until Cosima and I came back down the road. They could watch us a long way from there. They would know that everybody drives fast on that stretch. They had only to wait. Now, could anybody from this house have done a thing like that without your father knowing? Without his help?"

187

"No one," said Elena tonelessly.

"That's what I thought."

The girl looked at him for a long time without speaking. He was wrenched with pity for her, young and defenceless in the tangle of passion and intrigue. Her brother was dead. Her lover and her father had conspired to kill him. The lover had cast her off and she was left rootless and alone to be sold to a man like Tullio Riccioli.

"Now," he told her bluntly, "I think they may try to kill me."

"I know." She nodded wearily. "I heard my father talking to the men with the guns. If you try to leave the grounds they are to shoot you and say it was an accident. You should stay near the house. Do not go into the gardens or the olive groves."

"I'd like you to stay near me."

"Why?"

"Because I think I may need you. I think we may need each other."

Then he gave her another cigarette and made her stretch out on the sun-lounge beside him, and they lay back, watching Tullio Riccioli paint the blue sky and the grey trees and the flaring flower-pots in the bold and dashing style that had charmed the eccentrics of Rome.

Half an hour later, Orgagna appeared, dressed for the beach, a big coloured towel slung over his arm. He nodded a brief greeting to Ashley and Elena, then stopped a moment to admire Tullio's picture. They talked animatedly for a few moments. Then Tullio appeared to ask him a question. Orgagna cast a quick glance at Ashley and the girl, then turned back to Riccioli. After a moment, he patted him on the shoulder and walked quickly down through the olive trees in the direction of the cliffs. A moment later, Tullio turned round and made a quick gesture of triumph.

Ashley grinned and waved an acknowledgment. He was over the first hurdle. Tullio would take his message to George Harlequin in Sorrento.

Just before midday, Tullio packed up his gear and walked into the house. A few moments later, Ashley followed him, leaving Elena dozing wearily on the sun-lounge under the big umbrella.

When he reached his room, Tullio was waiting for him.

"Everything is fixed, my friend. I told him I wanted to go down to Sorrento and I asked him to let me have the car. Yes to both. He seemed happy to get rid of me. Told me I could stay the night if I wished."

"What did you tell him?"

Tullio smiled and shrugged in deprecation.

"What could I tell him but the truth? I am bored with these glum people. I would like to get out for a while."

"Fine."

Ashley walked to the wardrobe and fished for his wallet in the breast-pocket of his coat. He counted out five hundred dollar notes and handed them to Riccioli, who kissed them lovingly and waved them in the air before thrusting them deep into his trouser pocket.

"And the other five hundred when I get back? Right?"

"Right. Now repeat the message for George Harlequin."

"You have what he wants and you would like to see him as soon as possible. Anything else?"

"No. That's all."

Tullio giggled girlishly.

"Would you like to send a message to Captain Granforte as well?"

"No, no. George Harlequin will fix . . ." The words were half out before he had weighed their import. He saw Tullio's eyes narrow shrewdly, and caught the small frown that was hidden by the swift, practised smile. He had made a mistake. He could only hope that for the five hundred dollars still to come, Tullio might be prepared to overlook it.

"*Arrivederti, amico!*" said Tullio blandly.

"See you later," said Ashley tersely, and ushered him from the room.

Now he was really afraid. In the wooded confines of the Orgagna estate, between the tufa hills and the ancient sea, he was as surely imprisoned as in a dungeon or a police cell. The telephone was out of action. The high iron gates were locked. If he took to the orchards and the vineyards, the quail-hunters would flush him out and kill him, and swear that his death was an accident. If Riccioli failed him, then he was alone indeed.

He walked to the window and looked out. Elena was still there under the big umbrella. Cosima was standing talking to her. She was wearing a cotton sun-frock and a big straw hat and she carried a basket of flowers, fresh-cut from the garden. Far down the path between the orchard trees he could see Orgagna striding up, briskly, from his swim. Soon it would be lunch-time and, with Tullio gone, there would be only the four of them, a tense constrained little group, fearing and mistrusting each other, watched by the dour old steward who believed only in God and the house of Orgagna.

It was an unpleasant prospect, but somehow or other he would get through it. And afterwards, sooner or later in the day, Orgagna must make his next move. He couldn't afford to wait too long. Captain Granforte must soon make a move to claim his prisoner—to charge him with culpable homicide, or release him to print the big story.

He was hot and sticky from the sun. If he couldn't swim in safety, then at least he could shower before lunch. He stripped, laid out clean clothes on the bed and stood a long time under the jets, whistling a tuneless little song.

While he was dressing, he heard the sound of the car firing, revving up and moving down the long gravelled drive. It gave him confidence. It also gave him an appetite for lunch.

The meal was a much more elaborate affair than that of the day before. The servants had set up a large round table under a huge mushroom umbrella and beside it a long serving table at which Carlo Carrese presided. It was as if Orgagna had ordered a special display to make up for the absence of conversation.

The first course was an *antipasto* of astonishing variety and richness, matched with a bottle of dry white wine of the best Orgagna vintage. Then came the fish, small white fillets cooked individually over the spirit lamps and drenched with a rich red sauce of garlic and tomato and half a dozen exotic spices. Then the wine was changed to a rich red Barolo and the next course was brought on—*spiedini* in the Roman style—beef and ham and grated cheese and garlic and parsley, moulded into little shoe-shapes, skewered and fried in golden batter. Then, in drowsy succession, the pastry and the cheese and the fruit and the thick black coffee, with a good Napoleon to follow.

It was no meal for a summer's noon, but it served its purpose, and when it was done the two women retired to doze, while Ashley and Orgagna lay out under the umbrellas, side by side.

'Now,' thought Ashley, 'he will get down to business.'

But Orgagna seemed in no hurry to talk business. Instead he fished in his pocket, brought out five hundred dollar notes, folded them neatly in half and tossed them into Ashley's lap. He smiled, contemptuously.

"There's your money, Mr. Ashley. Tullio was wise. He decided that there was a better bargain to be made with me. You should be glad that I have saved your money."

"Thanks," said Ashley blankly.

Orgagna chuckled good-humouredly.

"For a man of your experience, Ashley, you are sometimes very naïve. Do you think a fellow like Tullio Riccioli will sell a rich patron like me for five hundred dollars? He can pick up as much as that for squiring a dowager for the week-end. But what happens when the dowager goes and you go? He is back to me. He knows it, believe me. He has earned twice, three times as much for the information that you are trying to contact George Harlequin."

Ashley said nothing. His head was swimming with the heat. His stomach was uneasy with the food and the wine and the brandy.

Orgagna said bluntly:

"Have you thought about my proposition?"

"The answer's still the same—no deal."

"You have the photostats, haven't you?"

"Yes." He could say it confidently now.

Orgagna heard the new note in his voice and looked up sharply. He said, deliberately:

"It's your last opportunity, Ashley."

"Go to hell!" said Ashley irritably.

Orgagna shrugged and lay back on the chair, hiding his eyes behind a wide span of glare-glasses. Ashley lay back, too. He felt dizzy and faintly sick. His palms were clammy and little beads of perspiration formed on his lip and on his forehead.

Then the pain hit him—a wrenching, griping agony in the pit of his belly that sent him lurching off the chair and staggering over to the balustrade of the terrace, where he stood, retching and gasping until the spasm passed.

"My poor fellow!" Orgagna was at his elbow, sympathetic and solicitous. "You're ill. Let me get you upstairs and out of the sun."

"Thanks ... I—I don't feel so good."

Orgagna took his arm and steered him hurriedly across the terrace and upstairs to his room, where he lay, sweating and knotted, waiting for the next spasm and the next, while Orgagna stood by, calm-faced but attentive, to help him to the bathroom and back again. Each time the cramps were more violent and the pain greater. His body was bathed in sweat and the room swam in front of his eyes. He heard Orgagna's voice coming from a long way off.

"How do you feel now, Ashley?"

He shook his head violently and the room slid back into focus. Orgagna was standing beside the bed, smiling down at him.

"I—I feel dreadful. Don't know what's the matter with me."

"You've been poisoned, Ashley," said Orgagna gently.

"Poisoned? I—I——" He tried to heave himself up on the bed, but the cramps seized him again and he staggered to the bathroom. This time Orgagna made no move to help but stood watching, a thin smile twitching the corners of his subtle mouth.

When Ashley came back, weak and tottering, to fling himself on the bed, Orgagna sat down on the edge of it and told him quietly:

"You've been poisoned, Mr. Ashley. The poison was in your dinner. It is a simple one, but very effective. The cramps are becoming more frequent, as you see. In an hour, two at most, you will die, painfully. There is an antidote, of course. Again quite simple. I am prepared to give it to you in return for the photostats—but not until they are safely in my hands. I suspect you may have left them at Sorrento. It is twenty minutes there and twenty back. It gives us time to administer the antidote, provided you are not too stubborn."

Weak and feverish, waiting for the next attack of pain, Ashley lay on the bed and looked up into the face of Vittorio Orgagna. There was no pity in it and no remorse. Ashley knew that he would sit there, calm and relaxed, and watch him die. The pain took him again and the journey across the rose-petal floor was twice as long and the return twice as uncertain.

He closed his eyes and tried to summon up enough strength to heave himself up and wrestle Orgagna out

195

of the room where at least he could call for help. Elena might hear or one of the servants. But when he tried to move, the nausea blinded him and the fever made his limbs as slack as string.

Orgagna's soft voice admonished him.

"I will watch you die, Ashley, believe me. You have thrust me too far along the road for me to turn back now. One man is dead—another is a small matter. And in this, there is less danger than you think. You are weak now, aren't you? You will be weaker yet and you will suffer more. I can give you the antidote any time you want, but I advise you not to leave it too long. Poison is subtle and unpredictable. Its effects vary with the subject."

Ashley lay silent and shivering, listening to him. He had no strength to argue. He must save it all to fight against the recurrent pain and make the lengthening journey across the room and back again. He could feel the fight ebbing out of him and fear taking possession of his racked and weakened body.

Four times the agony came on him and after each time the strength was less and the fear was more and the voice of Orgagna was more and more insistent.

Then Orgagna made his master stroke.

"The newspaper will pay for your funeral, Ashley. They will give you a two-line obituary and perhaps a citation in the Saturday supplement. But they will kiss the girls you have never kissed and drink the wine you have never drunk and live out the years you have never enjoyed. You're a fool, you know, a stubborn stupid fool. Where are the photostats?"

"Under . . . under the chest," said Ashley weakly. "The far corner."

Orgagna let out a long breath of relief and moved swiftly to the chest, lifting, as Ashley had done, with his shoulder. He picked up the envelope and let the corner of the chest fall with a thud. Swiftly he examined the photostats and then suddenly he threw back his head and laughed and laughed and laughed.

Ashley opened his eyes and said weakly:

"The—the antidote . . . for God's sake!"

Orgagna walked to the bed and stood over him, still laughing and tapping the envelope against the palm of his hand. Then he stopped laughing and his eyes darkened again.

"You know what I'm going to do now, Ashley?"

"You . . . you made a bargain."

"And I shall keep it. But then I shall telephone Captain Granforte and tell him that you are ill and troublesome, and that I can no longer take responsibility for you. I shall ask him to take you into custody and deal with you according to the law. Subornation, wasn't it? And culpable homicide."

"For God's sake, man! You've got what you want. Can't you . . .?"

Orgagna walked calmly to the mantel and pulled the big, plush bell-cord.

A few moments later a maid-servant came in and

stood goggling at Ashley lying on the bed with his knees drawn up to his chest. Orgagna spoke to her in slow careful Italian:

"Lucia, bring the *signore* three measures of castor oil. His dinner has disagreed with him." Then he grinned like a schoolboy and said in English, "It was the fish, Ashley. You got a bad piece. An old trick to play on the unwelcome guest. I must compliment Carlo on its success."

He went out laughing and Ashley buried his face in the pillow and cursed and sobbed in a fury of anger, humiliation and belly-ache.

I learned a lot from Louis as a correspondent; as a friend he gave me a lot. He was about the first of my Irish-English Catholic friends; and better friends than they I've never had. The Irish-English Catholics (one has to bracket them, they're so interwoven) cling endearingly, if a shade comically, to the mantle of martyrdom worn by their forerunners of penal times; they're cliquy, often, as are other groups conscious of persecution present or past; and their suave certainty of being personally on sure ground can sometimes seem a little smug. I, an infidel, loving them can gently laugh at them; knowing, though, that of all the Christians they are the most *Christian*; they may drink like fishes, swear like troopers, and practise, some may think, the most charming idolatries; but nobody practises so ungrudgingly the charity of Christ towards their fellow beings, Catholic, heretic or infidel; no other group of people is so free of malice, so understanding of human weakness, so unfailingly *kind*, so impulsively unselfish. The difference in this respect between such a number of the Catholics in England and the non-Catholics there, seems to me to prove that the Catholic Faith contains some powerful incentive to *goodness* not possessed, say, by the Church of England. Does it lie, perhaps, in the ideal of the *imitation* of Christ instead of merely praying to Him—an imitation which entails a love of people in fact as well as in church on Sunday mornings? And the tremendous belief that Christ re-appears in the flesh at every Mass must be a mighty inducement to strive after the imitation.

If I *had* belief I should want to become a Catholic—not too exact a Catholic; one must reserve some rights: a little like Don Camillo, perhaps—*monsignore ma non troppo*; and I should pray for grace enough to attain to one-tenth of the charity and human *goodness* which my Irish-English Catholic friends breathe out in their everyday lives as unselfconsciously as sweet peas their scent.

In October a cable called me home; and suggested I move to Vienna whence I should 'cover' the neighbouring Iron Curtain

CHAPTER TWELVE

NOTHING is so quick to take the starch out of a man's collar and the courage out of his soul as an old-fashioned bout of fish-poisoning. His body is in revolt, his mind is clouded with fever and weariness. He is an object of disgust to himself and of humorous pity to others. He is dosed like a child, starved like a dyspeptic and condemned to slow and queasy hours of recovery.

The best he can do is wait it out and try not to be too angry with himself. But Ashley had small patience at the best of times, and the thought of his physical degradation and his moral defeat was no help to him.

The grinning maid came in and fed him with castor oil. She pulled off his shoes and drew the coverlet over him and left him with a bottle of spa water and his own unhappy thoughts for company.

The big story was wrecked now beyond salvage. By a simple psychological trick, Orgagna had turned defeat into a trumpeting victory and had made his enemy an object of laughter for his folly and his cowardice. Now he was preparing the final humiliation, handing him back to Captain Granforte, as a fellow of no consequence, to be dealt with by the pettifogging routines of the law.

As he sweated the hours away between the bathroom and the lengthening periods of relief, Ashley tried to marshal his last remaining evidence against Orgagna. It was a personal thing now, a grudge fight, with no high principles to justify it. He wanted to convict Orgagna of murder.

The more he thought about it, the less he liked his chances. The only solid piece of evidence was the phone call from the Villa Orgagna to the barman, Roberto, and the money paid to him to report the movements of Cosima and himself. The rest was conjecture and speculation. He doubted that even Roberto could be brought to tell his story in the witness-box. For the rest, what did he have? Carlo's attempt on his life? It was unsupported testimony. Even if it were supported, there would be the adequate explanation of a father defending the honour of his daughter. The quail-hunters? A laughable fiction, matching the other fiction that Orgagna had tried to poison him, when any fool with half an eye could see that it was fish-poisoning. Cosima? No help there. No hope either, ever again. Elena Carrese? She, too, would look to the main chance, like all the rest of them. She had given him the photostats, truly. But he had lost them again. He had failed her. So, in this land where poor and beautiful girls were tuppence a dozen, she must look for the best bargain she could make. And Orgagna's was still the highest offer.

George Harlequin? He, too, had his ends to serve.

He was concerned not with moral issues, but with the delicate balance of forces in the European cockpit. Orgagna was more important to him than a gad-fly correspondent. Whichever way he turned, there were swords at his throat and mocking faces behind them.

He gave it up. He lay, clammy and miserable, on the big four-poster bed and dozed fitfully.

It was late when he woke. The light outside was softer and the air in the room was cooler. His body ached and he felt listless and uneasy. He looked at his watch. Ten past eight. He could not lie here like this, crumpled and clammy. He sat up and worked himself slowly off the bed. When he stood up his head spun with weakness, but he steadied himself a moment and the nausea passed. He walked slowly across the rose-petal tiles and turned on the bath.

The warm tub refreshed him and, although he was weak and faint, he dressed carefully in dinner clothes, spending a long time over the set of his tie which refused to come right under his unsteady fingers.

He lit a cigarette and tried to smoke it, but the taste sickened him and set his head whirling again. He stubbed it out and cleansed his mouth with mineral water. Before he walked out of the room he took a long look at himself in the glass.

His face was drawn and haggard. His skin was blotched and grey and there were dark, bluish patches under his eyes. His lips were bloodless and the lines about his mouth and temples were deeper than ever.

'I'm getting old,' he thought. 'Too old to be beating my heart out in this huckster's trade. I'll talk to the office and get them to give me a job at the desk—a nice, respectable job where a man can chew on his pipe and jibe at the youngsters and tell them about the big stories of the old days—and the bigger ones that got away.'

He heard the sound of a car coming up the driveway. He went to the window and looked out, forgetting that his room faced across the sea, away from the entrance approach. No matter. It might be Captain Granforte. It could be Tullio Riccioli returning from his afternoon hunting among the tourists. Either way, there was no hurry. He would give them a little time to settle themselves, then he would go down.

He pushed open the casements and walked out on to the narrow balcony with its curlicued iron railing.

The sky was peach-coloured now. The air was cooling with the coming of the small night wind that made a husheen-ho in the brittle leaves of the olives. The outlines of the tufa cliffs were muted to grey monotone and deep shadows lay in the narrow re-entrants where thin spirals of smoke rose from the cooking fires of the peasants. The sea was red with the last sunset touch, and the tiny fleets of the fisherfolk were rowing out towards the grounds. A faint haze hung over Capri and the windows of the high villas flashed gold and crimson across the strait.

The tourists would be sitting out in the bright little square and the donkey boys would be lopping homewards and the girls would be flaunting the new clothes in the ritual *passeggiata*. A man was a fool to break his heart straining after bylines and digging into the dirt of twentieth-century history, when he might enjoy all that for the price of a boat-ride. But folly like that was hard to mend. It was hard to turn back on the long, stony reaches of the crooked road.

Well, he was near the end of it now. It promised him nothing but humiliation and defeat, but he was too weak and tired to care. He turned away from the island and the sea and the soft sky and walked downstairs to the drawing-room.

They were all there—Orgagna, Cosima, Elena Carrese, Tullio, Captain Granforte, George Harlequin and old Carlo moving among them with a tray of cocktails. They looked up as he entered and he caught the little shock of surprise when they saw his grey, drawn face. Orgagna greeted him coolly:

"Kind of you to join us, Ashley. Are you feeling better?"

"Thank you, yes."

"Please sit down. Carlo! A drink for the *signore*."

"No drink, thank you."

He found his way to a chair, eased himself carefully into it and nodded a greeting to the others. Nobody spoke to him though they were all watching him, uneasily, over their glasses. Carlo finished serving the drinks and the olives and then stood back against the wall, the model of unobtrusive service.

"*Salute!*" said Orgagna.

"*Salute!*"

They all drank. Orgagna put down his glass and wiped his lips carefully. He looked at Ashley. He looked at Captain Granforte. Then he began to speak:

"We are all aware, I think, of the business which has brought us together. All of us, in one fashion or another, have been involved. I felt it wise, therefore, that all of us should be here at this—this closing stage. My reason is simple. In fairness to every one of us I feel the matter should be closed today, so that we may go about our business—important business to some of us—free of suspicion and unhappy after-taste. Captain Granforte agrees with me in this. That explains his presence here this evening. If there are questions to be asked, they should be asked now. If there are charges to be made, now is the time to make them. If there is evidence to be given, it should be offered freely and fearlessly. Do I make myself clear?"

He looked around at the little company, but none of them met his eyes. They were sipping drinks or nibbling olives or fumbling for cigarettes. Orgagna went on:

"All of you know why Mr. Ashley came to Sorrento in the first place. For some months he has been investigating my political and financial activities in the hope of finding material which might be used against me at the coming election. He came here to buy from a certain Enzo Garofano photostat copies of what were supposed to be letters from my private files. On the day of his meeting with Garofano, he also met my wife, whom he had known in Rome before she married me. They went driving together. On the way home, with Ashley at the wheel, Garofano was run down by the car and killed. Captain Granforte felt that there might be grounds for criminal charges, but, in deference to my wishes and in fairness to Mr. Ashley, he permitted him to come here as my guest, pending further investigations. Do you agree with all that, Mr. Ashley?"

Ashley looked up. He grinned crookedly.

"No comment."

Orgagna looked across at Granforte, shrugged significantly and went on:

"I had thought to do Mr. Ashley a courtesy, and at the same time to save embarrassment to my wife. But, since coming here, Mr. Ashley has put himself beyond courtesy. He has tried to bribe the members of my household as he bribed Enzo Garofano. He tried to make love to my secretary and then charged her father with attempting to kill him. When he saw my peasants out shooting—for his own dinner, incidentally—he claimed that they were forcing him to stay inside the grounds under threat of killing him. This afternoon he claimed that I tried to poison him, when as everyone can see he was suffering from nothing more than food-poisoning, simply cured by three measures of castor oil. Under these circumstances, I feel that I am excusde from further courtesy and I must ask Captain Granforte to relieve me of—of a very unwelcome guest."

Orgagna sat back in his chair and waited. George Harlequin lit a cigarette and smiled blandly at the tense little company. Captain Granforte looked down at his soft hands for a moment, then he looked at Ashley.

"Mr. Ashley, you are not obliged to answer any questions other than those I put to you in the privacy of my office in the course of an official interrogation. However, it would help us all, I think, if you were prepared to waive that privilege and answer some questions here and now. Would you do that?"

Ashley thought about it a moment, then he answered.

"Yes. But I reserve the right to decline any question."

Granforte nodded.

"That's quite reasonable. Now, the first question. Why did you begin this investigation of the affairs of His Excellency?"

"I belong to a news-gathering organisation. It's my job to investigate matters of public interest."

"*Ebbene!* Your action was not influenced in any way by your previous friendship with His Excellency's wife or your present feelings towards her?"

"No."

"What was the nature of the documents you were attempting to buy from Enzo Garofano?"

"They were six photostat copies of letters dealing with dollar transactions, the allocation of American grain-seed to distressed farming areas and certain bond-holdings in America."

"Did you in fact buy these documents?"

"No."

"Did you take them from Garofano without payment?"

"No."

Captain Granforte paused and licked his lips. His moon-face was touched with a faint smile of anticipation.

"His Excellency has made a statement to me claiming that during the—er—incident at the hotel, his wife saw you take certain documents, or an envelope containing documents, from the pocket of this man's coat. Is that true?"

"No."

Granforte turned quickly to Cosima.

"Did you tell your husband that, *signora*?"

"Yes."

Ashley could see it coming, but he was too tired to care. Sooner or later they would get at the truth and the truth would be just as dirty as the lies that were told to cover it.

Granforte turned back to him.

"How do you explain this discrepancy, Mr. Ashley?"

"It's quite simple. Cosima was lying to protect me."

"Thank you. I am glad you did not attempt another lie. Now . . ." He put his hands on the arms of his chair and pushed his soft body upright against the padded back. His soft mouth was smiling no longer. "Now if the lady lied once to protect you, is it not probable that she lied again—on a more important matter?"

"I don't understand."

"I think you do. She lied, as you lied, about the killing of Enzo Garofano. He was not thrown from the cutting, Mr. Ashley. He was walking up the road like a simple citizen going home. You saw him and you accelerated and you ran him down. You took the documents from his brief-case and gave them to the lady for safe-keeping. You brought them up here to use for blackmail. And this afternoon, fearing that you had been poisoned, you were induced to return them to His Excellency, who has now passed them on to me."

Like a conjurer pulling a rabbit out of a black silk hat, Granforte fished in his breast-pocket and brought out the brown manila envelope and tipped the six photostats into his hand.

Ashley gazed at him with amazement.

It didn't add up. Nothing added up. Orgagna was selling out Cosima as well as himself. That was feasible —a delayed revenge that would make him look like the wronged husband and maybe give him a fillip with the women voters. Journalist and wife conspire to ruin saviour of Italy. It might work. Orgagna had subtlety enough to think it out and gamble on it.

But the photostats? Read in conjunction with the typescript which was already in Granforte's hands, they were a damning indictment of Orgagna and all his works. Unless—and nothing was impossible now—Granforte had been bought, too, and George Harlequin was party to the whole devious transaction.

Granforte was still watching him, the light of triumph in his limpid eyes. Ashley struggled to get his voice under control before he asked:

"Do you mind if I look at those?"

To his surprise, Granforte made no objection but passed the envelope across to him. He spread the photostats out in his hands like a pack of cards and looked at them. They had nothing at all to do with the business operations of Orgagna. They were six harmless letters taken at random from the files and photostatted. He put them in the envelope and handed them back to Granforte.

"Well, Mr. Ashley?"

"They're the wrong letters."

Granforte spread his hands in a gesture of tolerant patience and smiled.

"What you mean to say, Mr. Ashley, is that Garofano was trying to cheat you with the sale of worthless documents. You did not know that, of course. If you had known, you would not have conspired, both of you, to commit murder and ruin the husband of the woman you love. When you found you had been cheated you turned to blackmail, to break this marriage and make profit out of it."

Ashley looked across at Cosima. Her face was buried in her hands. He looked at Orgagna, but he was staring straight ahead with blank, expressionless eyes, the very image of a wronged and grief-stricken husband. He looked at Elena Carrese. She was staring at Orgagna, her eyes bright, her hands clasping and unclasping in her lap.

"Have you anything to say, Mr. Ashley?" Granforte's voice was soft as silk.

"Yes, I have!" The words came out, rasping and dry, with all the strength he had left in him. "You're seeing this the way you want to see it, because you've all got an interest in concealing the truth. But you're going to hear it just the same. Those letters are a lie, a clever plant. The real ones I gave to Orgagna this afternoon. They were given to me by Elena Carrese because she believed that Enzo Garofano, her half-brother, had been killed by conspiracy framed in this villa and by this family. He had brought them to the hotel and given them to her for safekeeping during our negotiations. When we quarrelled and he ran out of the hotel, she still kept them, knowing he would come back. But he never came back. I can't prove what happened to him, but I believe he was hustled into a car and driven up here. I know, for certain, that Roberto, the barman, telephoned this place to tell them when Cosima and I had left the hotel. I say they waited for us to come down the mountain road, knowing that we would drive fast, as everybody does. I say they threw him under the wheels of the car and that Cosima and I were the innocent instruments of murder."

Granforte seemed unimpressed with the passionate outburst. He said coldly:

"Who is 'they', Mr. Ashley?"

"Orgagna as the organiser, the man with the alibi, the man who lifts a telephone and has things done by his faithful retainers. Carlo Carrese as the man who directs operations. Any two of a dozen peasants on the estate for the rest of it."

Granforte smiled ironically.

"You tell a dramatic story, Mr. Ashley. Professionally, I should say you were very competent. I am interested to see how you prove it."

"First, question Roberto at the hotel and see if you can get him to tell you about the telephone call from the Villa Orgagna and the man who paid him ten thousand lire."

"We shall do that, Mr. Ashley. Next?"

"Next ask George Harlequin here and he will tell you that I didn't have the photostats in my possession at the hotel, and that I didn't know where they were."

"Mr. Harlequin?"

George Harlequin's mild eyes were full of regret. His boyish face was wooden. He shook his head slowly.

"I'm afraid I can't help you much, my dear fellow. I know you told me you didn't have them. I know you told me you didn't know where they were. But that doesn't prove anything, does it?"

"Next, Mr. Ashley."

"Ask Elena Carrese. She will tell you how the photostats came into her possession. She may tell you why, but I'd advise her not to." He shot a quick, warning glance at the girl. "Then she will tell you how her father beat her yesterday and how, for her own reasons, she decided to hand the documents over to me. She pushed them under my bedroom door last night."

"What have you to say to that, *signorina*?"

Without a moment's hesitation she gave him the answer.

"Every word of it is a lie. I have not seen my brother since before I went to Rome. All I know of documents is what I have heard here and from His Excellency. This man tried to make love to me yesterday in front of the shrine and when I refused him, he threatened to—to embroil me in this matter. I am His Excellency's secretary. I have access to his papers. He was trying to frighten me. Then—then my father came and I was able to free myself . . ."

She broke off, bright-eyed and angry, and Ashley saw her flush with pleasure at Orgagna's sidelong glance of approval. It was clear enough now. With Cosima removed, there was still a chance for her. Orgagna could be won back. If he could not be won, he could be blackmailed. It was a sweeter victory than the one she had planned, because there was still hope in it. But he could not let it pass without a challenge.

"Listen, Granforte . . ."

"Please, Richard!" It was Cosima's voice, weary but

strong, raised for the first time in his defence or her own. "Don't say any more. Not here, not now. Whatever you say, they will twist and turn until it means what they want it to mean. I have tried to warn you before, but you would not listen. This time ... please!"

For a long moment, he looked at her and saw the pain in her eyes and the fear and the weariness and the wounded, disappointed love for him. Now, at last they were allies, and he hated himself that he had come so late to the wisdom of it. He turned back to Granforte and said simply:

"What now, Captain?"

"On the evidence at my disposal," said Granforte slowly, "I have no alternative but to place you both in custody on a charge of conspiracy and murder."

"I see." He stood up. The others watched him curiously. "In that case, I'd like to phone my office in Rome, have them contact the Embassy and arrange legal assistance."

Granforte nodded thoughtfully.

"Do that, Mr. Ashley."

As he walked to the phone, Orgagna said sharply:

"Isn't that a little unusual, Captain?"

"It is a courtesy," said Granforte smoothly. "In the circumstances, it would be unwise to deny it."

Ashley dialled the Sorrento exchange and booked the call to Hansen.

"*Urgentissimo*. It is a—a diplomatic matter."

The girl told him it would take half an hour. He

213

thought it would probably be longer. He put down the receiver and walked back to his chair.

"Half an hour delay."

"We can wait," said Captain Granforte.

For a moment it seemed Orgagna was going to protest. Then he clicked his fingers and Carlo Carrese began slicing lemon peel for a new round of drinks. They sat like strangers in a theatre foyer waiting for the bells to ring. But there were no bells, only the remorseless ticking of an ormolu clock on the big marble mantel, carved with the arms of Orgagna.

CHAPTER THIRTEEN

"CARLO!"

They looked up, startled, at the small, imperious sound of Cosima's voice. The old man straightened and looked to her.

"*Signora?*"

"Ring for Concetta, please."

Carlo walked to the bell-cord and tugged it. A few moments later there was a knock at the door and Concetta came in. She looked round, startled at the circle of tense faces, then turned to Cosima.

"*La signora vuole qual' cosa?*"

"My handbag, Concetta. The big brown one. In the second drawer of the bureau."

"*Subito, signora!*"

She bustled out, self-consciously. The others looked at Cosima as if anxious for some explanation of the banal little act. She paid no attention to them, but reached for a cigarette. Captain Granforte was on his feet instantly, offering her the light. Then he sat down again.

Carlo began shaking the new cocktail. The ice rattled dryly in the shaker, drowning out the ticking of the clock. Still nobody spoke. What was there to say?

Nothing that could be framed in the polite hypocrisy of words. . . .

'. . . I have cheated and won. You have cheated and lost. I have indulged myself no less than you; but your passions have betrayed you, while mine have turned to profit. You have lied and I have lied. My lie is accepted as truth. Yours will put a noose around your neck. We are all venal. We are all traitors. We are all potential murderers. Some of us are a little more skilful and ruthless than others. . . .'

Then, suddenly, Orgagna spoke. His voice was terse and irritable.

"Can we not end this, Captain? The situation is embarrassing for all of us."

"Most embarrassing for me, Excellency," said Granforte mildly. "I beg Your Excellency's patience."

"Very well."

Then Concetta came in with the handbag, cast a hurried look round and went out again to regale the kitchen with the odd behaviour of the *signori*. Cosima opened the handbag, took out a small gold compact and began to powder her nose. The others watched her as children watch the animated dummies in a shop-window. Cosima took no notice of them. Calmly she finished the little ritual, snapped the compact and put it back in her bag.

Carlo was decanting the drinks. Cosima summoned him again.

"Carlo!"

"*Signora?*"

"A moment, please!"

He seemed to hesitate a moment, then he put down the shaker and the glass, wiped his hands carefully on the napkin and came to stand in front of her, a tall, commanding figure, full of the dignity of age and faithful service.

Cosima looked up at him. Her voice was gentle and affectionate.

"Carlo, as you have heard the Captain say, I must soon leave you. It is the custom—a good custom—to reward a good servant. You have been my husband's servant, but you have served me, too; and I am grateful. Here is my gift."

She took from the handbag a thick white envelope and held it out to him.

The old man hesitated a moment and looked uncertainly towards Orgagna. Orgagna nodded briefly. The old man took the envelope, bowed stiffly and said:

"*Mille grazie, signora!*"

"*Prego!*" said Cosima and watched him walk back to the serving table, holding the envelope uncertainly in his hand. When he reached the table, she spoke again, more loudly this time, and more imperiously. "Open it, Carlo!"

The knotted hands fumbled uncertainly at the flap of the envelope while the others watched, in tense surprise. Granforte was leaning forward in his chair, his hands on the arms of it, as if ready to thrust himself forward.

Slowly, the old man opened the envelope and brought out a small wad of newsprint photographs pinned together. He was too far away for the others to see the subjects. All they saw was the heavy sepia ink of the popular Italian pictorials and the black captions underneath. Carlo Carrese turned them over slowly, one by one, his lips spelling out the captions. As he deciphered each one, he would look first at Elena, then at Orgagna, then at Cosima and back once more at the photographs.

The others watched him entranced, as if he were an actor miming the gamuts of emotions, shock, disbelief, fear, disgust and finally a slow, smouldering anger. Then the miming stopped and the actor gave voice—a deep, slow voice spelling out the simple question.

"*Signora*, will you tell me what this means?"

"It means," said Cosima, with cold precision, "that the man you have nursed as a child, whose father you served, whose house you kept, whose honour you have tried to preserve with murder, has taken your own daughter and made her a *putana*. He has not done it secretly. Her name and her face have been published in the press. The men who write these things have made a subtle joke of it so that all the world may know. Ask her yourself, if you do not believe me!"

But there was no need to ask her. She was cowering back in her chair, her face chalk-white, one bunched hand held to her parted lips. For one shocked moment it seemed as if the old man were going to stride over to her and strike her.

But the moment passed. Carlo Carrese's hand trembled and the clippings dropped and fluttered on to the serving table. He turned slowly and picked them up. He stood a while, bowed and uncertain, his weathered face twitching. Then he straightened up. His mouth was set, his face was composed. When he turned round they saw that he held in one hand the little bundle of clippings and in the other the short, bright knife with which he had been slicing the lemons.

Slowly he walked across the floor to Orgagna.

His Excellency stood up. They might have been father and son, except that the son wore the dress of rank and the father the livery of service.

No one moved. Not even Granforte. They were spectators in the pit. The stage belonged to the actors. They were remote, untouchable, playing out the last act of their very private tragedy.

Orgagna stood very straight and still, hands hanging at his sides, his evening jacket unbuttoned as it had been when he was seated. A pace away from him the old man stopped and held out the photographs. He said sombrely:

"Your Excellency will tell me whether this is true or not and I will believe him."

Orgagna's face was stony. His eyes looked beyond Carrese, beyond the others, beyond the panelled walls of the room—to what? To the final irony that mocks

219

all achievement? To the final truth that might wash out all the lies that had gone before?

"It is true," said Orgagna steadily.

In that moment, they saw the greatness in him.

There was a long pause. Not a muscle twitched in the craggy face of the old man. His eyes were steady and he stood rigid as a rock. Then he opened his hand and the photographs fluttered to the floor. Then the grim lips parted and the voice that came from them was low and sad, yet terrible as a trumpet blast. Orgagna stood, eyes half-closed, like a man awaiting sentence.

"Always, since you were a child, I tried to teach you that it was the house that mattered and the name. Keep the house strong and no wind could blow it down. Keep the name clean and all the dogs in the world could bay against it till they burst. A man should keep his sins outside the house and keep his faith inside. I taught you that—as your father taught me. To preserve the house and to preserve you, I was prepared to kill my wife's son. I trusted you with my own child. You destroyed her, too, as you destroyed the name and the house."

Elena screamed and the others gasped as the knife came up, swift and sure, driving upward into the heart with all the weight of the strong old body behind it. Orgagna made no move to stay it, but took it full in the chest.

For one suspended moment of shock they sat there, seeing the old man, gaunt and terrible standing over the body of his master. Then they started forward.

Granforte's sharp command drove them back.

"Sit down! Sit down all of you!"

They sat rigid on the edge of their chairs watching him as he bent over the body, while George Harlequin, unbidden, went to the door and locked it, lest the servants came crowding in, and drew the heavy curtains so that no one could see from outside. Then he switched on all the lights so that the room blazed with the baroque splendour of the ancient name of Orgagna.

The old man was still standing in the middle of the floor, rigid as a cataleptic. George Harlequin took him by the arm and led him unresisting to a chair. Captain Granforte still knelt over the body of Vittorio Orgagna. After a while, he straightened up. His moon face was grim. His limpid eyes were hard as pebbles. Then he began to speak:

"I was expecting this—or something like it. I did not know how it would come, or what would lead to it. I could only wait and see. When it came, I let it happen because that was best for everyone, even for him." He looked down at Vittorio Orgagna with something akin to pity. "You ask me how I knew? From the typescript of your story, Mr. Ashley, I saw the nature of the information you wanted to buy. I understood the violence to which it could lead. Your friend Harlequin—and he is your friend more than you know—told me that the photostats were missing. A check in Sant' Agata revealed the relationship of Enzo Garofano with the Carrese family and with the house of Orgagna. A study

221

of the marital history of His Excellency gave me a dozen motives as well as a clue to the location of the photostats. When I went up to examine the cutting from which Garofano had been thrown, there were signs of a struggle, although the ground had been raked and the leaves scattered to conceal it. I found a shred of cloth from Garofano's coat and there were leaves in his shoes and the stain of a crushed orange on his soles. The barman gave me the full story, after a little persuasion, and my colleagues in Naples are still looking for a man from Naples who offered Garofano a lift from Sorrento and brought him here to the villa. It was simple enough; and it would have been even simpler if any of you had chosen to be honest with me. Now...!"

He stuck his thumbs in his belt and faced them, challengingly. There was something strangely sinister about this soft pudgy man who stood, undaunted by all the magnificence of the house of Orgagna, with the dead body of the master of the house at his feet.

"Now, you will listen to me, all of you! There is not one of you in this room who has not had his part in this death, or in the one which went before. The old one," he pointed dramatically at Carlo Carrese who sat bolt upright in the chair, his eyes wide and staring, his mouth slack, "who will suffer more than any of you, although I think he is less guilty than most. You, Elena Carrese, who have lied and cheated and connived at murder and extortion to hold a man who was tired of you. You, *signora*," his soft finger thrust now at Cosima, "who loved a man who was not your husband and whose afternoon under the olive trees was the reason for the death of Enzo Garofano. You, Mr. Ashley, because in the name of news, you were prepared to lie and bribe and so create the situation out of which all this comes. Even you, Tullio Riccioli, because you come scavenging round the rubbish of other men's sins in the hope of a profit for yourself. All of you are involved. Against each one of you I can invoke the law on one charge or another. So . . ."

He broke off and looked around at their tense, strained faces. Then he dropped his voice to a whisper and went on in a low, crackling stream of commands.

"So, when you leave this room tonight, you will forget everything that has happened, except that the old one has been in failing health for some time. He has been erratic and subject to fits of anger. Tonight, for no reason at all, he attacked the master with this knife, and before any of us realised what happened, His Excellency was dead." He gave them no time to question or protest, but hurried on. "And if you ask me why I tell you this, I will explain very simply. A week from now there is an election. An election on which the stability of this country depends and her hope of progress over the next ten years. On the result of that election depend employment for the workless, food for the hungry, education for the children, schools, hospitals, all that peace and stable government can bring to us. You will remember that. You will remember that a lie cannot alter what has been done and that the indiscreet truth may wreck everything of good that is still possible to be done. Do you understand?"

"No!" said Richard Ashley.

Granforte whirled on him.

"Why not?"

Wearily Ashley tried to explain it to him:

"Because you can never bury the truth so deep that it can't be dug up. Because you can never hide it so long that someone doesn't remember it. Because it's safer to get it out, over and done with, before it festers into a lie and corrupts more and more people. That's the trouble with this country. That's the trouble with Europe. Everybody knows the truth but not enough people try to tell it, except fools like me who get their heads beaten for their pains."

"Are you prepared to tell the whole truth, Ashley?" It was the flat precise voice of George Harlequin cutting across the rising flow of his argument.

"Yes, I am."

"About yourself and Cosima and Carlo Carrese and Tullio here, and me and Granforte, all the tangled relationships and still more tangled motives."

"I'm prepared for that—yes."

"But can you guarantee that it will be printed?"

Ashley looked up at him in surprise.

"You know I can't guarantee that. No one can. A newspaper works on limited space and caters for the daily reader interest. It's impossible to . . ."

"It's impossible to tell the whole truth, and you know it," said Harlequin bluntly. "It's the thing we're all up against, my dear fellow. Even if you could tell it, most people haven't the patience to read it or the courage to listen to it. They want headlines and they get headlines, because the headlines make life look nice and simple and uncomplicated—black and white, good and evil, farce and tragedy. But you can't run a country like that. You can't govern a nation like that. It's not a machine, it's people. And the only one who knows the truth about people is God Almighty. I'm not sure that He's very happy with the knowledge either. Why not be reasonable about it? Let the dead bury their dead. And if you don't want to bury the truth, why not let it sleep a while? Who's the loser? Not you. Not..."

Abrupt and nerve-shattering the telephone rang. Ashley leapt up to answer it. Captain Granforte barred his way.

"Let him go, Captain," said George Harlequin. "Let him do what he wants."

Granforte stepped aside and Ashley stood with the receiver in his hands, listening to the crackling, impersonal voices saying *"Pronto! Pronto! Pronto!"* all the way up to Rome, and looking down at the dead face of Vittorio d'Orgagna and the blood that spread out over his white shirt-front. The *'prontos'* started again in descending scale—Rome, Terracina, Naples, Castellammare, Sorrento—and finally, Hansen came on.

"Pronto! Hansen speaking."

"This is Ashley . . . Sorrento."

"Great to hear you, Ashley boy! Great, great! What's news?"

"I've got the Orgagna story. All of it, beginning to end."

"You have?"

"Yeah. At this moment I'm standing in . . ."

"Kill it," said Hansen succinctly.

"What?" He stared stupidly at the receiver.

"Kill it. Take a week off and enjoy yourself. Then come back here."

"But . . . but I don't understand. This is big news, Hansen. Orgagna's dead. He . . ."

"The biggest news at this end, sonny boy, is that Harold P. Halsted, President of the *Monitor* chain, has been appointed U.S. Ambassador to the Republic of Italy. Therefore, all Italian scare news from this source is out. O-u-t! Out! He's Ambassador now, but he still underwrites the pay-cheques. Didn't you get the note I sent you with the money? Don't you read the papers? Where've you been all this time?"

"On a story, remember? The Orgagna story."

"Yeah. I remember. Seems you missed some of the angles, doesn't it?"

He heard Hansen chuckle boisterously and the line went dead in his ear. The others watching him saw his face crumple and shrink like that of a child about to burst into tears. The receiver was still in his hand when he turned round and said stupidly:

"They—they killed the story."

"I would have told you," said George Harlequin, "if only you'd given me time. I've had a watching brief on it for months—as I've had on you."

"When a man is dead," asked Granforte of no one in particular, "why is a story so important?"

But Ashley did not hear him. He stood there, with the receiver in his hand, staring into the black mouthpiece until Cosima came and took him by the hand and led him to a chair beside her own.